Books by Reneé Porter

Bell Park

The Dreamville Series
Dreamville
Gordon's Dreams

The Taliaferro Chronicles
The 13th Victim
Redemption Ridge
An Inquisition of Angels

Gordon's Dreams

Dreamville II

Reneé Porter

Roet Press   Plantation, Florida

DEDICATION

For Rob - Hello, Sweetie.

CHAPTER ONE

I awoke from a nightmare, reaching across the California king bed to find if April's body was there, alive or dead. When I found the tendrils of her dark curls stretching across the pillows as if in search of me, when I heard her quiet, small breaths, I buried my face into her hair and breathed in the scent of it.

She lived.

So vivid had the dream been that I knew that only the intolerable illness from which I suffered could have induced such a horrible nightmare, one where I could savagely assault her and then . . . then place the barrel of a gun between her breasts while she watched me, loved me, as tears rolled down her cheeks.

My movement in the bed toward her sleeping form must have roused her from her own deep dreams and she rolled to me and buried her face against my shoulder, embracing me and returning to whatever slumbers from where she had stirred.

I could not return to my own sleep and I feared that I would once more slip away into that nightmare world where I had destroyed the only valuable part of my life. As I lay there with the warmth of her sleeping body lying half draped over my own, I began to wonder if she was indeed safe with me.

I had dreamt of her "other" life many times, but I had always been her hero, her love. For the first time in the year we had been together, I had dreamt that I was the villain, death come to claim her. The thought that I could harm her, the thought that I could take her life away made me physically ill. I'd sooner leapt from our Manhattan terrace onto the pavement below than hurt her. Fear gripped my heart as I wondered if my illness could truly cause me to do those things in the waking light or harm her in my sleep.

Anxiety came in waves. I could feel my breathing

quicken at the remembrance of the dream I could not shake off. I closed my eyes and tried to count to focus on anything other than the thought that I could hurt her. In the darkness of the room, only the feel of her lying with me kept me from running away from her and hiding in my office.

As I felt her heart beating softly against my chest, I began to calm and could feel my own heart slowing its wicked rhythm. I wondered, and not for the first time, if she were safer away from me. I could smell the lavender scent of her hair and wanted to be strong enough to keep her safe, but if I lost control . . .

I pulled her closer to me and began to kiss her eyelids, her cheeks, and finally her lips. I remembered crushing her cheek in the nightmare and shivered. No, I would never do that and I wiped the image from my mind.

In the barely moonlit room I could see only a scarce outline of her face on my shoulder. It was my intimate knowledge of her body that led me to touch her carefully, softly, the smooth skin of her breasts pressed next to my bare chest.

I should have allowed her the luxury of her sweet

dreams, but I was still so panicked from the nightmare that I desperately needed to touch her, to love her, and to feel her responsive body against mine.

She swam upward from sleep and returned my kiss and smiled. Wordlessly, she pulled me closer to her own living, breathing body, seeking out every space on my body that she knew so well, bringing my love inside her and driving away the madness of the dream.

We moved together in the quiet night without speaking and as we grew closer to the conclusion of our lovemaking, I remembered the dream and placing of the gun against her tender chest. I tried to forget the nightmare, to think of her as she was now, clasping and rocking with me, kissing me as she brought me to completion. I fell into her arms, this time burying my face against her chest instead of a gun.

She stroked my hair as I lay upon her and she wrapped her long arms and legs around my body, cradling me and unknowingly pushing the darkness from my mind with just her caresses.

Only she could drive the demons away that were produced by my illness. I knew that she was aware of my need for her, for her comforting love. As she held me, I thanked God that I had only dreamed of her death and that she was really there with me. Alive. Breathing. This time I knew I would be able to finally fall into a deep and dreamless sleep.

For months she had suffered through my delusions that she had another life, one that she called "Dreamville", the world where she was with me sometimes and not with me at other times, where she and I had shared such a confusing relationship that there were times when I woke wondering if "Dreamville" was a delusion or real. I thought of one of the "Dreamville" versions of a life with her that consisted of nothing more than work or the occasional dinner with our families, a world where I had never kissed her and had watched her with disinterest, a world where she barely knew my name or of my existence and I damned my illness again.

In reality, after several months of renewing our acquaintance, her love broke down the walls I had built around myself, I finally found the courage to tell her of my illness, my delusions, and my fear of loving her or anyone else lest she reject me. I was unprepared for her response. She had said that it did not matter.

"I've known you forever, even when you say you had

rough times. Why would I fear you now?"

And in that aspect, she was right. I had known her since high school, had been best friends with her oldest brother who now worked with me, had watched her from afar as even then I was suffering the effects of my illness.

She had not known then of the early diagnosis, the doctor visits, the medications, or the secretive "vacations" to visit family in Scotland that my father had arranged. What little she knew of me then, at least what I thought she knew, was that I was just another annoying teen-age friend of her brother, someone from her school who seemed to be around her family's house a lot. She didn't know that I was there, more often than not, to see her – Pamela April Norris, the object of my first male desires, the object of my first and only true love. Unknown to me at the time, she later told me that she had watched me as well.

I told her that I never knew, that I thought that she disliked me and that I was just another awkward boy who was often hanging around her house. She was always reading. I had never understood then why she was always reading and never dated. But that was then, before we both changed.

At the time we were both driven apart by outside forces that kept us away from one another for over eight years. She to university and I . . . I simply trying to save my own life. I did go to work for my family eventually, although university was not a choice. But when it came to the delicacies of business, of being able to see trends in business, to understand financial forecasts, especially to the surprise of my family and my parents' relief, I thrived, somehow able to separate the delusions from reality.

It was only when I was in social situations, especially with other women, that I found myself floundering. I couldn't love them and more than once I had called them 'Pamela', unable to separate the "Dreamville" of her from the real world. I called her Pamela then, before we were together. Only her family called her April and I never was brave enough to even call her Pamela in those early years.

I had even briefly engaged myself to a beautiful, blonde English rose named Charlotte whose thorns came out when I told her of my illness. At first she had stayed, fooling both herself and me that she could live with the situation, but she could not. Our relationship was not good for me. She had what I thought of as some rather unhealthy ideas about sex, ones that to this day I was still embarrassed in which I had participated with her.

When I began to pull away from the more bizarre aspects of her sexual tastes, she called me a prude and began to belittle me for everything, especially my illness. She became cruel when she found me in my other worlds, especially my Dreamville life where I wanted only Pamela April Norris. Charlotte finally left me when she told me the thought of passing on my damaged genes to her children nauseated her.

I was not surprised. She had enjoyed the benefits of my family name and money, but when she began to push me away, I knew the relationship was nearing its end. I was not sad. She was not my first love and in my heart, I knew I had never really loved her and that I could never love anyone else but Pamela.

When a chance meeting with Rick Norris occurred after those years had passed, I used it to discover where his sister was and how the course of her life had gone. I had believed that she had gone on to some happy existence with a husband, family and career where I was only the vague memory of a tall, skinny boy with an accent.

When I discovered that she still lived in the same

Connecticut town where we had grown up, that she was still single and unattached, I leapt at the opportunity of just seeing her once more. With the inheritance from my grandfather, from which I somehow managed to make even more money, I found a way back into her life again. And, though the rest of my family was always there to observe my actions, to make sure that I was not dangerous to myself or anyone else, they surprisingly were silent about my attachment to her.

Originally, my father had brought my mother and myself to America because of my illness and the distance of my family's home from the care he knew I would need. As a physician, he knew how fragile my health could be. So I was free in my own way, especially in my business enterprises, but nevertheless watched and minded. I may have been the head of the company, but I still had to answer to others.

I had no idea of how much April's presence and her love would come to impact my life in the coming year, the year we were 25, the year we had found the love I had never dared to hope to find with anyone, much less with her. After all, as Charlotte had so well demonstrated, not many women are willing to commit themselves to an ill man, especially a man who was schizophrenic.

CHAPTER TWO

I slept late and awoke the morning after the nightmare alone in our bed. I laid there and listened to try to hear her movements in our home. Nothing. I remembered the dream again and quickly threw the covers from my naked body when I remembered our lovemaking. I closed my eyes and took a deep breath. She was okay. I had not raped her or hurt her. I had not shot her. I counted slowly to ten to stem the panic rising in my chest and began to feel the fear subside.

She could have gone out for breakfast or coffee or she could be somewhere in the apartment where I could not hear her. I grabbed clothing from my armoire and went to the shower to wash the stink of the fear-sweat from my body. I wanted more than anything to go through the house looking for her, but I had to gain control over myself, not to be afraid, to trust her love.

When I had showered and dressed, I allowed myself to leave the bedroom. Part of my mind was terrified at what I might find and part of my mind struggled to control that fear. I took a deep breath and began to concentrate on the methods I had been taught for controlling my delusions through reality testing. Schizophrenia came in many different degrees of incapacitation. My form was, while nevertheless schizophrenia, was one that could be monitored and even at times, recognized by certain truths within my daily life – for example, an orange glass Christmas ornament, orange pekoe tea, a specific, yet simple, cartoon Santa on a shopping bag, or the appearance of a man called Will in my study. He often seemed to be both friend and nemesis, a man whom I had painfully learned to recognize as a hallucination.

I walked into the living room that she had been slowly redecorating over the past few months and found her sitting in my favorite brown leather club chair, her legs dangling over one arm, one hand holding the front page of the Times and the other holding a bright red Fiesta Ware coffee mug.

She was wearing my white shirt from the night before and little else other than the simple white cotton underwear that she insisted on buying. Frugality was her biggest fault in my eyes, which was not really a fault, but I was afraid to let her know just how her normalcy made her perfect in my eyes. I had offered to buy her fine silk undergarments and she had refused, saying that the lace itched and the silk was a ridiculous waste of money and time.

I had pointed out that she did not have to wash her own clothes, but ever the sensible and thrifty woman, she had looked at me strangely, and then had thrown her arms around my neck and laughed, telling me that she couldn't imagine sending her underwear out to be cleaned.

She had been appalled by the fact that I had not even owned a washer and dryer.

"You mean you send everything out to be laundered?"

"Well, yes," I stammered. "I didn't want anyone here other than to clean weekly and I just found it easier."

She had laughed and then dragged me out to purchase a washer and dryer, cleaning supplies, and appliances I could not imagine ever needing, including a German iron that did seem excessively expensive, but which she said she had to have as well as a custom made ironing board to accommodate her height.

It was all confusing for me. I had grown up in a house with servants and had never seen the inner workings of a household even after we had moved to America. When I had held up a small mesh bag and asked what its purpose was, she took it from me and told me I didn't need to worry about it.

"It's for my undergarments. No one touches them but me," she said.

I had leaned in and whispered "And me" and we both had smiled.

Now after almost a year together, I was beginning to understand her and trust her.

"You've already dressed for the day," she said and smiled at me. "I'm being lazy this morning, though I did make coffee."

I grimaced and went into the kitchen to pour a cup of her coffee. Weak and watery as usual. I liked strong coffee, the type I could get on Calle Ocho in Miami, coffee so thick it poured almost like syrup.

I had never liked weak coffee or tea, a fact she told me that she found amusing in someone from the British Isles. Even when I reminded her that I had spent part of my life in America, she still called me her "Scotsman" and begged me to take her to my family home there, a topic I had successfully had evaded thus far.

As I carried the mug of weak coffee into the living room I saw that she had stretched out on the long leather sofa and had spread the newspaper around her on the floor, the table, and her lap. I walked over to her, kissed the top of her head and slipped the front section of the Times off her lap.

"Hey, no fair! I was reading that. I got up first and even made coffee for you."

"April, I love you more than life, but this," I said as I held up the mug, "is not in any way, shape, or form — coffee." And I sat down in the chair she had vacated for me, just barely dodging another section of the paper that she lobbed my way.

"Fine. Fix your own damn coffee from now on."

She threw the rest of the paper in the floor and

stomped off toward the bedroom. I knew she wasn't really angry. The "coffee" debate had been raging since she first moved into my home. And I was just so happy to see her safe and sound that the banter made me as happy.

I heard drawers in her dressing room being closed loudly and then the slam of the bathroom door off our bedroom. This time I couldn't resist the impulse to follow her.

I put the undrinkable coffee down on the side table and hurried to the bedroom, undressing as I went. By the time I reached the shower, I found her sitting on the marble bench, waiting for me.

"Took you long enough," she said.

I entered the shower and lifted her up to me, grasping her buttocks, lowering her onto me and leaning her against the shower wall to support our bodies as we kissed and slid rhythmically against one another. The water from the shower was like making love under a waterfall and I leaned down to lick the warm water from her erect nipples.

She grabbed the back of my hair and pulled my mouth to hers, deeply exploring it with her tongue. As I felt myself getting closer to the edge, I slowed our pace, and lowered her onto the wide marble bench.

I withdrew from her and she moaned, reaching out to me as if to say "Come back." I turned the shower control and adjusted the water to a fine mist that began to fill the glassed in shower and returned to her waiting body.

As I tasted her salty-sweet skin, she raised her arms above her head, closed her eyes and surrendered to me. We were drawing out our lovemaking as long as we could bear. By the time we could hold back our desire no longer, I re-entered her pulsing body and we began to move together faster and faster until we both came, almost unable to see one another in the mist that had filled the entire bathroom.

I propped myself up on my forearms to look at her smiling face through the thick mist, her dark, wet curls forming a perfect frame around her face.

"April, I need to tell you something. I need to tell you now so you won't be frightened. You trust me now, don't you?"

I didn't realize that there was a slight tremor in my voice as I spoke, but she heard it and knew I needed her trust now. She looked into my eyes and I remembered the same trusting look from the dream and I wanted to stop what I was about to do. I feared everything at that moment, especially losing her forever.

She reached up and softly touched my cheek.

"Tell me, Gordon. It's okay. Just tell me."

I sat up and propped her long legs across my lap, stroking them as she continued to lie flat on the cream marble bench. I took a deep breath and looked out into the mist that filled the bathroom. I suddenly hoped that she could not see my face as I began to tell her about my dream.

She was silent throughout my narration and I wondered for a moment if she were really there, if I had really made love to her or if the entire episode had been one of my forays into Dreamville.

I looked around the bathroom for a cue as to whether what had happened had been real or a product of my altered mind, but I could find nothing.

"Gordon, I'm here."

She sat up cross legged next to me and laid her head on my arm.

"I'm here."

I sighed again. As much as I had enjoyed our passion, I realized that I had told her my dream, waited for her to leave and nothing had happened.

"I'm not afraid of you. You had a nightmare, not a hallucination. There's a difference, you know that. Besides, you've never been violent with me. You've never given me a reason to be afraid of you."

I looked away from her. I couldn't watch her expression as I asked and I had to ask.

"What if, what if I did . . . do something or hurt you?"

"No. You don't get to ask what if. You love me. I love you. I mean, what if Manhattan sank or the sun exploded? No. I love you. I'll always love you. Don't make up reasons where there are none."

I pulled her onto my lap so that she faced me and I held her as close to me as I could without our bodies merging once again. She kissed me and smiled.

"What would Dr. Fritcher say about the nightmare?"

I paused and thought about the little doctor with his awful orange pekoe tea.

"He would say the nightmare was more about my insecurities than my illness. And then he would make me drink that awful tea."

She laughed and stood before me, taking my hands and placing them on her breasts and pulling my fingertips down the front of her body.

"This is all me, my lovely Scotsman who hates tea. This is real. Not the dream nor Dreamville nor mysterious women who try to hurt me. This is real. Me. Real. Standing here in front you like a drowned cat, but still real.

I leaned my face against her flat belly and could hear her breathing, feel the dampness of her smooth skin against my cheek.

"Come. Let's get dressed and get out of here today. Do you need to go into the office or can we take a day off and maybe go to MoMA? I feel the need to see Van Gogh today," she said.

I nodded my head and laughed. She had to see "her" Van Gogh at least once a month. I remembered the first time she dragged me to the Museum of Modern Art to stand in front of Van Gogh's *Starry Night*. I had spent more time watching the play of emotions upon her face than I had looking at the painting. She had talked about the painting, but I had heard nothing. If I had not been sure of my love for her before that moment, I was then.

"Yes, I can skip work today, though your brother will probably tell me I have a thousand things to do."

I followed her from the misty bathroom into the bedroom and as we dressed I thought of something else that we had not discussed in the past year.

"April, do you think I should tell Rick about things, about my illness? I feel unfair putting the burden of company decisions on him sometimes. He's a good man and he's been truly decent about our arrangement."

She looked at me quizzically.

"Whose arrangement?"

"Ours, April. Most men would not want their sisters living in sin. I'm sure he feels protective of you. And your family. Damn, your father probably wants to kill me."

She pulled a lavender v-neck cashmere sweater over her head and began to twist her hair into a knot at the nape of her neck.

"My family has no say in this, including Rick and my father. God, Gordon, living in sin? Where did that come from? It's not 1950."

I shrugged my shoulders and pulled on my trousers. My illness and her family's ignorance of it had worried me as much as our lack of a formal commitment.

"April, you hae na . . ." I felt the Scottish burr slip out and stopped. "You have not told them, have you?"

"No, I have not. You need to trust me as much as I trust you, Gordon."

She left the room and I could hear her gathering up the newspaper and carrying the mugs into the kitchen. What would she do if her family objected to her being with a man who was, well, not quite sane? Would they insist she move out? Would Rick quit? Would they separate us?

Even with the interference of Dreamville in my mind, she had kept me calmer and happier than I had ever been. Could I bear to lose her? Would I become a crazed stalker who would hurt her if she left me?

I shook my head as if to rid my mind of the idea of harming her and the water from my own hair fell all over my shirt and trousers.

"Shit," I said louder than I had intended and April appeared at the door to see if I was alright. When she saw what had happened, she began to laugh and came to me and began to unbutton my oxford cloth shirt and unfasten my leather belt.

I felt myself stirring in my trousers and moved away from her. Sometimes her least touch aroused me and if I let her undress me, we would end up spending the day in bed.

Of course, she felt me harden beneath her fingers on the zipper of the trousers and dropped her hands to her side as I moved back.

"I'll let you dress and I'll rinse out the "awful" coffee from our mugs."

As she went to leave the room, I called out and stopped her at the door to the bedroom.

"April, please think about what I asked. I'm quite serious about this. I think your family should know about my . . . my problem."

She gave me a small smile and disappeared down the hallway. I wished that she would give me some sort of indication of how her family would react. She seemed to think it was nothing, but I knew it was not. If she were my sister or daughter, I would not want someone like me within 50 feet of her.

"You're borrowing trouble, Scotsman," she called out from the living room.

I felt my brow furrow at her words. How did she do

that? How could she tell what I was thinking or sometimes anticipate my actions? Sometimes it felt we had been together 25 years rather than just a year.

"Call my brother and get going. I'd like to see Van Gogh before the afternoon crowd discovers it.

CHAPTER THREE

Rick, of course, was irritated when I told him I wouldn't be in the office that day.

"Gordon, we've got a lot to do today and this is Friday. I have no desire to work over the weekend. Tell my sister to remove her nails from your arm so you can come into work."

I smiled at the notion of April's nails on my bare skin. It was not a thing that Rick would want to really imagine.

"Rick, I know you can take care of everything today and no working over the weekend. I'll see you Sunday afternoon. April and I will be going up to your family's for dinner. We need to talk with everyone about some things."

Rick was strangely quiet on the other end of the line.

"Alright. But, if you don't like my decisions, you can't fire me. I warned you."

"Rick, I have no worries about your work and you have no worries about being fired. We'll see you and Lisa and the family on Sunday."

April walked into my office just as I finished the conversation with her brother.

"Sunday? Dinner? Oh, Gordon. Don't do this. It's not necessary and it's not their business."

I leaned back in my desk chair and looked up at her.

"Oh, no," she said. "Don't look at me with those grey-blue eyes of yours. You're not going to change my mind. I am not going to Connecticut on Sunday."

I remained silent and smiled at her beautiful face. Small dark curls had escaped from her knotted hair and made her pale skin look like silky cream.

"God damn it, Gordon! This is something we should discuss first. You don't get to make this decision by yourself!"

Her face flushed red now and she left me sitting in the office alone. She was right. I should have discussed it with her first. But she was also wrong. I strongly believed that her family should know.

Less than an hour later we were standing in front of her Van Gogh. I stepped back across the exhibit room and sat down on a low bench to watch her. She would tilt her head in the direction of the whirling sky and study the areas of blank canvas that Van Gogh has used as a milky white rather than paint. She had posited once that perhaps he could not afford the paint, but for all her love of the painting, she never researched the artist's techniques in creating it.

She came to join me on the bench just as a small group of people were beginning to form a loose circle around the painting.

"I can't believe I lived so close to this painting for most of my life and never knew it was here."

She sighed and looked off toward the door. I knew where we were headed next – Edward Hopper's small *Gas* painting with colors so vibrant that it looked as if it had just been painted. She would then drag me down to the Jackson Pollack paintings where she would lose herself in Pollack's *Full Fathom Five* and its pull of the viewer through the depths of the water it represented, from the lighter navy tones at the top to the dark inky blackness where the layers of paint covered matchsticks and other detritus.

I did not like the Pollack portion of her visits to MoMA. The wall sized painting to the right of *Full Fathom Five* was difficult for me to be near. Perhaps it echoed the confusion that seemed ever present in my mind. But at least she did not drag me through the Picassos and their twisted faces.

I preferred the calmness of the Met, especially the large Egyptian room with the pool of water surrounding the Greek style buildings and their Napoleonic graffiti. The galleries of the Met calmed me, but the crowds there were too large, even in the mornings, so we rarely went there.

Her love of New York's museums was only matched by the quiet streets of the Village and our weekly excursions to The Strand bookstore. Again, it was always crowded and I often escaped to the small café next door while she worked her way from the first floor and upward. The café had good coffee and fresh croissants and I sat and watched the people walking by as I waited for her to exit The Strand, her arms usually full of books.

Her love of books was beginning to overwhelm our apartment and I finally gave in to her idea of turning two of the larger guestrooms into a library with a sliding ladder on an oak rail that ran around the large room. It was her favorite room in the house and the six months it had taken to renovate had been interminable. It became the one room in the house that I knew that I could find her if I didn't hear her anywhere else in the house.

But today, she skipped both the Hopper painting and the Pollack section and laced her fingers in mine, leading me toward the exit of the museum. She had been very introspective this morning and I suspected it might have something to do with my insistence on the Sunday dinner in Connecticut.

Outside the museum, our car was waiting for us and she leapt into it and slid far across the red leather bench seat. I joined her and directed the driver to head downtown toward the Village.

"April, I can't live this way anymore. I can't take it any longer, your family not knowing. The one thing I've learned in living with my . . . illness is that truth is the strongest weapon I have to fight it."

She looked down at her lap and brushed imaginary

lint from it.

"I know. I think they'll understand. They know how happy I've been. But they'll also be concerned. The broken arm last fall, the hospital visits. I'm afraid they'll think a pattern of abuse has formed."

I winced at her statement. She had been thinking about it as well. Although the hospital visits had all been the results of accidents and I had not been part of them, who knew if her family would see it that way?

She moved across the leather and embraced me. I pulled her closer and was about to kiss her when I stopped and pushed the intercom to tell the driver to head up the Hudson River Parkway instead. I pushed another button and darkened the partition between the front and rear of the car and began to roll her down onto the leather seat.

"Gordon, I haven't made out in a car since, well come to think of it, I've never made love in a car. Is this a good idea?"

I didn't answer, but pulled her slacks down and pushed her cashmere sweater up, revealing her braless breasts. I dove into the space between her breasts and began to take turns kissing and gently nibbling at each nipple.

She began to undo my belt and unzipped my pants, releasing me and stroking me. I wanted to suddenly rip her pants off, but she sat up and pushed me back into a sitting position and straddled me, kissing me.

I leaned back against the seat and closed my eyes as the pull of her lips against mine was almost more than I could bear as her body rubbed against me.

I didn't want to stop her, but I did, knowing how close I was to coming. I moved her back onto the bench and ripped the pants away from her hips. I smiled when I saw the white bikinis covering her. She made even the cotton panties look sexier than the flimsiest lace thong. I pulled at the panties and lifted and parted her legs as I thrust myself into her.

I could vaguely hear her boots against the rear right window and I knew that the car was shaking with the power of our lovemaking, but I didn't care. All I could think of was pushing into her as deeply and as hard as I could. She used the leverage of her boots against the window to raise her hips even higher and match my thrusts with more power than I had ever felt from her.

Just as I released myself, she pulled my mouth onto

hers in order to stifle the cries of her own climax. I could feel sweat trickling down my back under my clothes and though we were both overheated from our exertions in the back of the car, neither of us could separate ourselves from one another.

After what seemed as if an eternity had passed, I began to withdraw from her and redress her and myself. She was still lying on the seat as she held up her shredded slacks.

"Hmm, I think we have a problem."

I looked at the pants in horror. I had torn them apart in my haste. Had I been that violent with her?

"My god, April, I'm sorry. I didn't realize. I didn't hurt you, did I?"

She laughed and tossed the pants at me.

"I think we were both fairly intent on one thing only and the state of my clothes was not high on our list of priorities."

I leaned back against the seat and watched as the countryside passed by. How could I lose control with her? It ruined the afternoon for me. It could be a sign of things to come. This could be something that could not be stopped and it had to be stopped. I had to protect her.

The image of the gun from the nightmare flashed through my head again and I could feel the throbbing of a migraine coming on.

"Gordon, they're just pants, not the Shroud of Turin. We just need to find something I can wear to exit the car."

I tried to smile so she could not see my fear and pushed the intercom button directing the driver back into the city and to Macy's.

"I'll run in and find something for you, if you don't mind waiting in the car."

"Well, I don't think I'll be going anywhere else in just my sweater and boots. You might as well pick up some underwear while you're at it. These are gone, too," she said holding up the cotton bikinis that were in two pieces now.

"Good god, I didn't mean to rip everything off of you. You just . . . oh, hell, I'm not sure what I was doing or thinking after a certain point."

"Oh, I think I know when that point happened," she said and slipped her hand back into my trousers. I could feel myself stiffen at the touch of her fingers and I reluctantly withdrew them from my trousers.

As much as I wanted her, I could not chance losing control again. The back of the car was soundproofed and our driver would not hear her if I began to hurt her.

"If we start that again, I may not have anything to wear into Macy's to get your clothes."

"Okay, okay. Besides I'm getting hungry. Tell Ralph to go by Benito's after we leave Macy's. I'll call in our take-out while you're replacing my clothes, though I'd give good money to watch you shopping in the lingerie department at Macy's."

She giggled and laid her head in my lap. I stroked her hair which had escaped from the knot and now flowed down her back. By the time we reached Macy's, she was sound asleep and I covered her with my jacket so she wouldn't be exposed as I exited the car.

Now, if only I could get through Sunday. If I didn't find myself hallucinating. I stopped for a moment before I entered the store and looked at the car sitting there, knowing that she slept inside. Only two days and my happy ever after could disappear. Was I even more insane for insisting on telling her family? I hoped I was doing the right thing. Only she and my family knew about my illness. I was taking a big risk in telling her family. I decided that I needed to see my own father before continuing down this path. And I knew what he would say. Oh, did I know what he would say.

CHAPTER FOUR

As I expected, my father was not happy with my decision to tell April's family about my condition or with my increased devotion to her.

"Gordon, you've forgotten how hard the "Charlotte" episode was. Stress always makes your condition worse and this would be very stressful, especially if they objected to your relationship after discovering the truth."

I started to interject that this was different, but he stopped me.

"Yes, I know she knows and she says it doesn't matter, but think about it. What if you tell her family and they disapprove? What if they convince her to leave you? Can you bear that?"

No matter how much I tried to get a word in, he was ready to answer before I asked a question. He had obviously seen how attached I was becoming to April and had been preparing for this moment for quite some time.

"What if Pamela Norris reveals your secret to the world even if you survive the eventual break-up? Think of what that would do to our company."

"Stop it!" I stood and went to the door.

"April would never do that. I came to you as my father, for advice, for your support, not as a physician or lectures on the past."

He sighed and stood behind his desk.

"You thought other women would never do that and how much did it cost the family? But forget the money. How much did it cost you? Almost a year of therapy and withdrawal into our home in Scotland that left you almost a ghost of yourself."

"I should never have come here," I said. "I should never have told you. I'm not a child anymore who has to be minded and watched. And call your watchers off. I am in control and you know it."

He walked around the desk and placed his hand on my arm.

"The fact that you say you are in control says that you are not. You know the limitations of your illness. I don't want to find you off your meds again and locked away at Burnock because some woman has money on her mind more than your well being."

I jerked away from him. I had not been so angry in such a long time. Why did he keep comparing April to other women? If I couldn't make him understand, could I make April's family see that I would never hurt her?

"You're wrong," I said. "I'm stronger than I've been in years and the fact that I recognize that I am ill should tell you that."

"I'm not giving April up because you're worried about money. And do I need to remind you that I've known her and her family for almost half my life? She's not Charlotte!"

He stepped back and raised his eyebrows.

"Do you realize what you just said?" he asked.

I had had enough and I left, slamming the door behind me. He could cause me problems financially. He could take my company away. After Charlotte, the family had taken steps to quietly make him a conservator of my money. He would be the reason I would end up living in the highlands around Burnock again, not Charlotte.

I stopped midway to the elevator and realized that I had said and thought the name Charlotte and not April. Did he know something that I didn't? My head began to pound again. I rubbed my temples as I waited for the elevator. Why had I thought of Charlotte's name instead of April's?

I stretched out one arm to support myself against the wall next to the bank of elevators. Was I losing control? Was reality one step closer to another visit to Dreamville? Was it a portent of things to come?

No, I thought. He was wrong. He could take everything from me and April would still be there. No matter what he or April's family had to say. She was not like Charlotte. I had to believe that.

When I arrived home, I found April sitting on the terrace watching the setting sun surrounding her in yellow light as she sat staring out across the park.

"Gordon, I didn't hear you come in. Where have you been? I tried your cell, but it went to voice mail. I was beginning to wonder."

I sat down in the large chair next to her and looked out at the darkening city around us. I knew that she had almost said "worry" instead of "wonder", but that she had stopped herself in time.

"I turned my mobile off," I said as I loosened my tie and unbuttoned my shirt.

She waited quietly. She knew I would tell her. She took my hand in hers and squeezed it gently.

"I went to see my father. He's . . . Damn it!"

"He's what, Gordon?"

I removed the blue silk tie and tossed it on the table between us.

"He believes that I'm making a mistake by moving our relationship forward. He was adamant that I not reveal my illness to your family."

She leaned forward and took my left hand in hers.

"Maybe he's right. Gordon, why the sudden urgency to reveal this to them? Does it matter? Shouldn't how we feel matter more?"

I sighed and leaned away from her, withdrawing my hand from hers. I really couldn't explain why I felt the need to tell her family. Maybe it was the dream.

I looked around for any of the familiar "totems" that might be signaling an episode and saw none. God, my head felt like it was going explode.

"Okay. We'll wait. I'll follow your lead on this. I've got some papers to take care of and then I think I'm going to crash for the evening."

I leaned over, grabbed the tie, kissed her forehead and headed to my study. I actually was going to take something stronger than an aspirin for my headache, but I didn't want to worry her any more than I had today.

And, of course I should have known what was coming, but I had had a good couple of months handling things. I should have known, should have remembered that there was no cure for my illness, not even her love and faith. But, when I entered the study, there he was – my old friend, Will. My nemesis, Will. My hallucination.

"Well, she certainly has you under control doesn't she?"

I turned my back to him and tried to remember that he did not exist, that he was a delusion.

"Oh, dear God, don't try and ignore me. I'm here with you and you know I'm not going to leave any time soon. You might as well listen to me."

I still ignored the voice behind me.

"Fine. But remember I'm everywhere. I see everything. And I see that she's firmly controlling you.

Look at your journal, if you don't believe me. Look at what you wrote yourself."

I grabbed the medication from the drawer, swallowed it quickly and left the study, taking care to lock the door as I left. I was surprised to see April standing in the hallway, watching as I locked the study.

"Told you so," Will's voice said from where he now stood next to me in the hall, unseen by her.

I knew April was watching me stare at the wall and knew that she could see that I was struggling not to speak.

I took a deep breath and looked away from Will.

"I'm going to sleep in the guest room, tonight, dear. Please understand," I said and left her staring at my retreating back.

"Uh oh, here she comes," Will said. "Looks like she's not giving up. Maybe you can get a little slap and tickle from her."

"Shut up!" I finally screamed. I couldn't take any more of his voice.

I felt April's hands at my back as she had rushed to me when I began to yell.

"Gordon, no, come to bed with me. It will be okay."

"April, I have loved you for so long and so much and I believe that you feel the same. I know that your presence is not a hallucination or that I am currently lost in what you call 'Dreamville'."

"But, I am afraid I may hurt you. He's here and I don't know if I can handle him and this stress right now. I'm afraid the dream from the other night might have been a warning that I'm about to lose control."

I had told her about all my "totems" - my warnings that I was slipping backward. She knew what I meant when I said that "he's" here. I had thoroughly described Will and the effect he had on me. I had told her that he was the worst of the hallucinations, a ribald, sneering bully who in the past had caused me the most problems.

My head was throbbing and I buried it in my hands. I could feel the changes coming and the thought of hurting her made it worse.

"April, please! Leave me be!"

She moved in front of me and placed her hand on my shoulder. I violently pushed her arm away and accidentally knocked her down. She stared at me with tears in her eyes, the same look on her face from the dream.

"Gordon, don't. Please," she said, her voice trembling.

I stood over her and shook my head.

"I can't risk it. You need to leave me. I'll hurt you. Hell, I just did!"

"No, Gordon, what's wrong with you? This is my home, too. I love you. You love me. Please don't push me away."

I left her in the hall and went to our bedroom and threw her luggage upon the low bench at the base of our bed and began pulling her clothes from the closet and stuffing them into the luggage.

She stood at the bedroom door and no matter how much she pleaded with me or how much I wanted to go to her and comfort her, I could not. My father was right. I could never have a permanent relationship with anyone, including her.

I closed the Louis Vuitton cases and threw them off the bench.

"Take them and leave now. Just go!"

"But Gordon, where do I go? This is the only home I have now."

"Damn it, *Charlotte*, I don't care," I said as I sat down

on the bed and rubbed my temples. My head was exploding and I was beginning to see small bursts of light when I opened my eyes.

I hadn't realized I had called her Charlotte, but she had and she rushed across the room and began to slap at my head and arms.

"Fuck you! I'm not Charlotte! I'm not leaving. She left, but I'm not!"

She continued to beat at my shoulders and arms weakly and I grabbed them and threw her down on the bed, shoving her legs apart, intent on punishing her the way Charlotte had liked. I could feel the anger welling up inside me and I raised my fist to hit her when I heard Will's voice.

"That's the way, boy. Show her who's in charge. Hit her hard enough and then take her the way you used to have old Char. Teach her a lesson!"

The sound of his voice shocked me back to reality and I saw what I was doing, that she was not Charlotte and that this was something I did not want.

She slid out from under me, grabbed the luggage and ran from the room to the elevator.

"April, wait, please come back. I'm sorry," I cried

out.

But I couldn't stop her and though I had called out to her, I made no attempt to follow her. I laid down on the bed and felt as if my heart were going to burst from the pain in my chest and my head.

I had just lost the love of my life, the only woman who had loved me without reservation. And I had driven her away. I thought then that I had to return to Burnock. I had nowhere to go, either. Not without her in my life.

CHAPTER FIVE

When I awoke the next morning, I found that I had slept in my clothes, that April wasn't there and I relived the awful details of what I had done. Last night had really happened.

I rubbed my face and walked to the bath to shower before I began to pack to leave for Burnock. I sat on the marble bench and thought of making love to her there just the other day. I don't think I could have felt any worse than I did. I ran my right hand across the smooth marble, wishing that she was there, that my hand was touching her soft skin. I don't know how long I sat there, but it seemed as if time had just stopped. I kept waiting for Will to reappear and do his "Told you so" routine, but the delusion was over for the time and had only lasted long enough for me to lose April.

After packing, I called my father and told him the whole sorry story. He was calmer than I had expected and said that he would meet me at JFK before I left. I had expected that response. I was being returned to my watchers full time, to my family estate, to the only refuge I could run to when the madness overcame me.

As Freddie pulled my car away from my New York home and drove me to the airport, I looked back in sadness, feeling foolish to think that I could have ever have had a life with April. Last night she had seen the madness and the danger and she had run just as "Will" and my father had predicted. I just hoped she was alright. I would have father make arrangements to sell the apartment and get her things to her, including a Hopper painting she had loved in the foyer. She could sell it or keep it. I hoped that she would keep it so that she would remember that I did love her once, maybe that I always would.

I thought about offering to send her money as well, but decided that she would see that as an insult. All she had ever wanted was love and money would sully that, cheapen it and make her feel like a whore and that I would never do to her. I loved her still. I would love her forever, but I decided I would never leave Scotland again. Scotland was home. Scotland was my sanctuary.

As I walked into JFK, I looked for my father's tall form among the many people passing through the different gates. I saw him near the British Airlines ticket counter and headed towards him. I was surprised that my mother had not chosen to meet me as well and then I thought of the many times that she had to do this and I understood why.

Just as I reached him, he turned and stepped back, revealing April standing behind him, her luggage already being checked and tagged.

"Father, this is not a good idea. I told you what happened. April, you need to leave. This will not work."

My father ran his hand through his graying hair and shook his head. April's face was impassive, revealing nothing.

"April came to us last night and told your mother and me what had happened, that "Will" had returned. I predicted that you would decide to leave New York for Burnock and told April so."

He placed his hand on my arm and squeezed it slightly.

"Son, she knows everything and she still refuses to leave you. I don't think I could stop her from following you if I tried. Perhaps I was rash in my assessment. Maybe it's too early to know."

It was the closest my father had ever come to addressing me as an adult and his touch on my sleeve was even more revealing. He had never touched or hugged me since I had left public school in England and we had moved to America. I knew that it wasn't because of my illness or because he might not love me. It was just his very reserved manner. He treated my mother in the same way. His upbringing had been old school, where men never publicly displayed affection or approval except for a pat on the back.

That he had touched my arm in one of the most public places in the world in such a difficult situation impressed upon me his determination to solve this problem.

"Father, April cannot go to Burnock. It will be difficult enough there as it is."

"Did you tell him that I almost killed you last night,

that I was not just having mild delusions, but that I was out of control?"

My father moved between us. Stern would have been a mild word for his expression.

"Gordon, please lower your voice. When I said she told us everything, I meant everything. Why do I have to repeat this? Should I employ someone to accompany you both on the trip? Can you control yourself long enough to arrive at Burnock?"

I lowered my head much as I had when he had scolded me as a school boy.

"No, father. No. I will be fine. But she still should not go. I implore you. I have no intention of returning to America. I plan to live alone, at home, and no longer be a burden or a danger to anyone."

"Gordon, that is exactly what you should not do. Living alone will only increase the delusions and hallucinations. Interacting with other people will help you more. She can help you cope with them so that you can return to New York."

"I will not have her act as a nursemaid," I hissed.

For the first time, April spoke. She moved beside my father and stared into my eyes.

"I will be no one's nursemaid. I can be your friend or your fiancée or whatever, but I won't be your nurse or maid. If it fails, then it will be a vacation to Scotland – at my expense, by the way, and not yours."

She was adamant and I could see that I could not change her mind. I turned to my father again, a last desperate hope for his assistance.

"Must she stay at Burnock? Can't she stay in the village? I can't say what will happen if I'm alone with her. It simply is unsafe."

"Which is why your cousins will be there, although they know nothing of your illness; however, the estate staff, who have all dealt with you in this situation before now, will also be present."

"No, she's to stay at Burnock as either your friend or fiancée. It's your choice. However, as the family has come to be aware of your relationship with her, I would think that the latter is more appropriate, especially with the ring you placed on her left hand."

I sighed and placed my luggage at check-in. I was not going to win this argument. I did not know who was more determined – she or my father.

I turned from them and began to walk to the security

check-in. I stopped at the end of the line and April fell in line behind me.

"She'll be returning alone," I said to my father. "I certainly hope you booked her ticket for an open return."

"She booked her own passage. As she said, she's paying for this herself. The only thing I have offered is our home and that she has accepted."

He placed his hand before me and I shook it hesitantly.

"Take care of yourself, son. I expect to see you again soon. Oh, and call your mother when you arrive at Burnock. She can fill you in on the details about your cousins' visit."

He turned to April and smiled.

"April, do not let him bully you, although I sincerely doubt that you will."

Then he laughed and hugged her and walked away. I was stunned by his actions. What had she told my parents that would win their favor so strongly?

"Close your mouth, Scotsman, and step on. The line's moving."

I looked into her dark eyes and frowned, but did as she said.

An hour later and 30,000 miles over the Atlantic, she had curled up in the first class seat next to me and her head had fallen against my shoulder in her sleep. We had barely spoken since passing through the security checkpoint at JFK. I briefly mentioned the layover at Heathrow and plane change, but she tersely informed me that she was aware of the connections necessary for the trip and then became silent.

I was very uncomfortable sitting next to her after my behavior the previous night. Truthfully, I was embarrassed. It was the only time I had actually tried to physically hurt her other than in that horrible nightmare.

Her head drooped further against my chest and I signaled for a flight attendant. She couldn't sleep in that position and I quietly asked the attendant for a blanket and pillow for her. As I waited for the attendant to return, I could not resist the temptation to brush a curl of her hair from her face. The touch of her body was electrifying and I quickly pulled my hand away.

She did not waken as her seat was reclined and the pillow and blanket properly placed. I realized that she probably had not slept the night before and was so exhausted that she would not wake until she had completely rested.

I reclined my own seat and decided to try to sleep myself. Before I dozed off, I reached out and took her hand in mine. God help me, I was so afraid to love her, but I could not help it.

CHAPTER SIX

I awoke in the apartment in New York and knew that I was either dreaming or hallucinating in Dreamville. Good God, would the agony of having April and being without her ever end?

I wondered what version of Dreamville I was in now. At least I was not a teen-ager. But was this the version where we were 32 and strangers or the version closest to reality where we were 25 and engaged?

There was an indentation in the pillow next to me so I assumed it was the version of Dreamville where we were together. I couldn't have been more wrong.

Just as I sat up in bed, Charlotte walked into the room with a tray laden with English breakfast food, including orange pekoe tea. Ah, well, there was the clue. The orange pekoe tea. I knew where I was. At least the signs told me. I wondered if I would wake up on the plane next to April or in some other world my brain travelled.

"Uh, Charlotte, this isn't necessary. Do you mind taking it back into the kitchen. I'd like to shower and dress. I have quite a bit to get done today," I said to her, although I had no idea what I was going to do.

She sat the tray on the bedside table and removed her robe, unveiling her naked and rather appealing body to me as she crawled into bed with me.

I quickly scooted across the bed and pulled a sheet around my naked body.

"Really, Charlotte, I do have to dress and leave. I don't have time for any . . . play."

She threw her hands back and upward and smiled a Cheshire cat grin.

"Even if I let you ravish me? I've been a very, very bad girl. You need to punish me."

She pulled a blue silk tie from under the pillow and waved it before me.

Oh God, I remembered that Charlotte had loved that

sort of lovemaking and it really was tempting. Her body was unbelievably voluptuous. I could remember how I had often taken her in rough love play. I was ashamed to find my body being aroused by the sight of the blue tie wrapped around her arm.

The smell of the tea suddenly permeated the room and I remembered that this was not real, that I loved April and that I wanted to find her now no matter the cost.

I quickly walked to the bath and locked the door behind me to keep her from following me. The thought of making love to her made me a bit ill. I saw the door handle turn and heard her voice from the other side of the door.

"Gordon, don't be ridiculous. We have plenty of time before we have to be at that dreary American antique shop. Open the door and come back and play."

Antique shop? Oh God, this was the version of Dreamville where I had introduced Charlotte to April. There was no way I was going to take Charlotte to April's store. I remembered the look on April's face the first time I had had this episode. I could not put myself through that again, even in a delusion.

"Charlotte," I called out, "I have to go into the office today. We'll do that another time."

I could hear her in the bedroom pacing on the other side of the door.

"Well, I suppose I'll have to go with your employee's wife. What was her name? Oh, yes. Lisa."

I pulled on a pair of trousers and rushed into the room. She could not go to April's shop. I had to stop her.

"Call Lisa and cancel. I'm not sure that it would be appropriate for you to be socializing with an employee's spouse and I cannot go and I cannot stay here."

She was sitting at the end of the bed with her legs crossed, nude except for my tie draped over her rather large breasts. I grabbed my clothing and went back into the bath to shower and dress.

I found her pouting in the large sitting room before I left to go to April's shop. She was still half dressed and drinking the awful tea.

"So sorry I can't stay. Why don't you putter about the house while I'm gone. You could make a plan, perhaps of what you think the place needs."

She ignored me and stared out at the terrace and I went to the elevator as fast as possible. As I waited for it,

I noticed the lack of the Hopper painting or the table which sat there in my both my real world and the other version of Dreamville. I winced, thinking of making love to April on that table and how much I missed her and how much I loathed Charlotte's presence there.

It took almost twenty minutes to get to Soho and April's shop. I prayed that she would be there. I wanted to see her so much, to touch her. I knew that this delusion was not real and that I was somewhere else in reality, but it did not help. All I wanted was in the room beyond the glass door where I stood.

As I entered, I looked across to the counter where April was cleaning a silver candlestick. When she glanced up and saw me, her face lit up with a smile.

"Gordon, I'm so glad to see you. I wanted to tell ..."

I didn't let her finish. I rushed around the counter and took her in my arms and kissed her as if I hadn't seen her in months. I craved the taste of her, the smell of her.

She stepped back from me and stared at me, surprised, then dropped the candlestick and returned to my arms and pressed her body against mine, returning my kiss as passionately as I had kissed her.

"Wow. I did not expect that," she said. "I was about

to apologize for being rude the last time we talked."

"Can you close? Can we go up to your apartment?"

She looked around, almost confused.

"Um, sure. It's early and we're here alone."

She started towards the door and I grabbed her hand.

"Wait, do you still have that antique iron bed in the back?"

"Yes . . . yes, just let me lock the door and put up the closed sign." She grinned as she rushed to the door just as two women entered.

Damn it! No matter what I did I couldn't seem to change this delusion from Dreamville. The two women were Lisa and Charlotte.

"Oh, April, I'm so glad you're here today," Lisa said and led Charlotte into the far side of the store.

April returned to where I stood at the counter. I could not let this happen again. I could not. I began to panic.

"Sorry. They shouldn't be here too long. I can lock up then," she said.

"April, leave with me now. Up to your apartment. Leave the keys for Lisa to lock up. Just go with me now,"

I whispered so that the other women couldn't hear me.

"Gordon, I can't just leave. It would be rude. . ."

"Now. Go with me now," I said, interrupting her.

Before she could respond, I saw Lisa heading towards the counter, followed by Charlotte. Too late.

"Hi, Gordon!" Lisa said brightly.

Charlotte moved forward and took my arm and kissed my cheek.

"Darling, I didn't think you were coming. I'm so glad you're here. I found a few things you might like, though most of the things are unfortunately American."

Charlotte turned to face April.

"Oh, you must be Lisa's family. I'm Charlotte, Gordon's fiancée," she continued.

I looked to see April's face first turn pale and then crimson with anger.

"Gordon's fiancée? Oh, well maybe you'd be interested in an antique iron bed I have in the back," she said staring at me and then turning back to Charlotte, she continued, "but then again, probably not as it's American. The shop is, after all, called Americana Applied."

"If you all will excuse me, you can lock up," April said handing the keys to Lisa. "I have a root canal scheduled, though it probably will be much more fun than this has been."

She glared at me and slammed the door as she left.

"Hmm," Charlotte said. "Well, Gordon, we can always shop at better places with more European things."

"Oh, will you shut up, you stupid twat!" I said and rushed into the street to look for April.

I ran to April's apartment building, but Frank, the doorman who seemed to appear in every version of Dreamville and in reality as well, refused to allow me to enter.

"Sorry, Mr. Stewart. She said no one was to come up, especially you. She was really upset. Crying."

"Frank, I'll give you $500 dollars to let me in. I have to explain something to her. For heaven's sake, please!"

He shook his head and just looked down at his feet.

"I could sure use the cash, but I could lose my job."

Then he looked up suddenly and continued, "but if I happened to step away from the door to pick up something, I wouldn't see anyone go up."

I pulled a wad of cash from my pocket and dropped it behind me where he sauntered over to look surprised at what he found. I rushed past him and through the door and hit the elevator button for her floor. How could I explain this to her? There was no excuse I could think of.

I pounded on her door and called her name. No response.

"April, I'm not leaving till you open this door!"

The door swung open and I could see both the hurt and anger in her eyes that were red from the tears she was still shedding.

"What? Humiliating me wasn't enough? You had to come here, too? Oh, Frank is so fired!"

But she stepped back and allowed me to enter her apartment.

"Don't blame him. Listen, I need to explain this to you. God, I wish I could turn time back. I'm sorry. I'm so very sorry. I became engaged to Charlotte before we became reacquainted. I'm so embarrassed. I should have broken things off with her and told you, but she just appeared and I didn't have time to say anything."

"You certainly had no trouble getting it out just now. Look, Gordon. I appreciate you giving Rick a job and I'm sorry I was rude in the past, but whatever you think, well, I'm just not the woman for it."

"I've made too many mistakes and I'm not going to

be hurt again. I'd rather be alone than worry about when the axe is going to fall. And I won't be second to any other woman. In other words, I won't be your mistress or whore."

She had calmed down and had placed the kitchen island between us. Why was this version of Dreamville so hard? I had to make her see that Charlotte was an aberration of the past, that she, April, was my future.

"April, please. I don't love her. I love you. I've loved you since we were kids. I would never have made a commitment to her if I had thought you were even the least interested in me."

She buried her face in her hands.

"Gordon," she sobbed. "Please leave. I can't go through this. It hurts too much. Please don't do this to me."

I went round the island and wrapped my arms around her as she shook with the grief that was racking her body. I held her as tightly as I could.

"Please don't cry. I do love you. I want to spend my life with you. Please don't tell me it's too late."

She laid her head on my shoulder and it felt so right. A few moments passed and then she looked up into my eyes as she wiped the tears from hers.

I kissed her and began to pull at her clothing. I cleared the kitchen island with one sweep of my hand. Our passion then was as strong as it was in my reality. I pushed her onto the island and ripped at her underwear the way I had when we had made love in the car on the Parkway.

"Gordon, slow down. I'm can't . . . Gordon, don't. Please stop. I can't do this now. Please. Stop."

But I could not. I tried to push myself on top of her and bring her hips to me, but she tried to crawl further from me, begging me to stop, and I saw that I was hurting her and I did pull away.

"My God, April. I'm sorry. I thought you wanted to make love." I backed away from her and she began putting her clothes back on.

"I want to make love to you more than you could possibly know," she said. "But I can't do this knowing you're committed to someone else. Oh god, please don't make me love you and then hate myself for loving you when you leave me."

I went back to her and took her in my arms again, holding her as if to convince her that everything would be alright.

"You really are the only person I've ever loved. You must believe me. You are my life, my love."

She sniffled and wiped the tears from her face and smiled up at me.

"You'll be the death of me, you know that, don't you?" she said.

"No, don't, don't say that. Don't ever say that," I said and I woke up on the plane, reaching out for her as the setting sun was coming in the windows of the plane.

"Gordon, are you quite alright?" she asked, but it wasn't April holding my hand. It was Charlotte.

CHAPTER SEVEN

Oh God, I was still in a delusion from Dreamville. Charlotte was not supposed to be on the plane with me. This entire delusion was new. I struggled to find a totem or clue as to what was happening, but I couldn't find anything. Charlotte was drinking coffee, not orange pekoe tea.

I looked around the compartment for Will and saw no one. This could not be real. April was my reality, not Charlotte. I felt boxed in and began to find it difficult to breathe.

Before I could say a word, Charlotte handed me an asthma inhaler.

"Dear, here, take a deep breath. The recycled air on

these planes is dreadful. No wonder you're having an asthma episode."

Asthma? I may have been schizophrenic, but I had never had asthma. Nevertheless, I inhaled deeply and the tightness in my chest began to ease.

"We'll be at Heathrow in no time. Here, take a drink of my tonic water and lean back and relax."

Heathrow? Good lord, this was even worse than the previous delusion. Why the hell was I on a plane with Charlotte that was landing at Heathrow instead of April? I glanced across the aisle and saw a man reading The Times.

"Excuse me," I said to him. "Would you mind telling me the date on that issue?"

"Why certainly," he said and moved the paper away from his face. I didn't know whether to be relieved or worried. It was Will, grinning impishly at me as he related the news to me the year and I realized that I was 23, not 25 or 32. Another visit to Dreamville. Just a different delusion this time.

"Who are you speaking to, Gordon?" Charlotte asked.

"Please tell me you're not having an imaginary

conversation again. This is really getting tiresome. What am I supposed to tell my family? You can't meet them behaving in this way."

I sat up straight in the seat and faced the movie playing out to its end as we neared the airport.

"No, you're absolutely right. I can't meet them. You're going to break things off with me before then. Now please let me close my eyes and get back to reality."

"Gordon, don't be absurd. I'm not going to leave you! Whatever made you think that? So what if you're a bit eccentric? You wouldn't be the first Englishman to be so!"

I leaned over and spoke lowly to her.

"First, I'm not eccentric. I have schizophrenia. An illness, not a personality trait. Second, I'm Scottish, not English. Please remember that."

She ignored me and then began gathering her things together for the landing at Heathrow. I closed my eyes and began to pray that when I opened them that I would really be awake with April by my side.

"Not going to happen, Stewart," I heard Will say from beside me. "Get ready for a really fun time with the lascivious Ms. Charlotte. Miles to go before you sleep and all that American tripe."

I cringed. This new visit to Dreamville was definitely not ending as fast as I wanted. I'll just keep my eyes closed and not allow anything to deter my journey back to April, I thought.

I was almost asleep when I felt the plane's wheels touch the ground. I looked out and saw the lights of Heathrow. Still here. Damn.

"Gordon, can you grab my carry-on from above? It has some of our more interesting, ah, items. We wouldn't want to forget it."

I pulled the case down and handed it to her. That was not one case that I was going to take through customs. Who knew what she had in it?

I was so relieved to have gotten away from the airport that I had no idea where we were going.

"Oh course you do, Stewart! You've been there many times before," Will said from the front seat where he sat next to the driver.

And he was right. We were deposited in front of Charlotte's Kensington home. I sighed as we walked up the steps followed by Will. He was not going to leave me alone, it seemed.

Charlotte's butler opened the door and she instructed him to pay the driver and to retrieve our luggage. She threw her gloves down on the table next to the door and removed her cashmere coat, dropping it on a settee that looked chillingly familiar to the one in the nightmare I had had of April's family.

"If you don't mind, would you sleep in the spare room tonight, dear? I'm absolutely jet-lagged."

I was filled with relief. I could escape her and perhaps even Will.

"No, not a problem. See you in the morning."

"That's what you think," Will whispered in my ear.

I ignored him. He was not real. This was not real. Any second I was going to awaken on the Brit Air flight holding April's hand.

"Not going to happen," Will giggled and bounced up the staircase ahead of me.

I entered the spare room and saw him sitting on the chaise longue next to the window.

"Go away," I said.

"Oh, don't be so grouchy. We're going to have so much fun tonight!"

"There's no way in hell that I'm sleeping with her

again. If this is just like the memory of when she dumped me, then she's going to do it in the morning. I seriously doubt anything is going to happen."

In a single leap he moved from the chaise to the bed.

"Oh, Stewart, haven't you realized that this isn't a memory? Everything old is new again, as the Yanks say," he giggled and disappeared.

I sat down on the bed and sighed. Why couldn't I wake up? This was going to be a bad night. I could just feel it and I switched off the light and lie back on the bed, waiting for morning to come and hoping that it would end this horrible visit to Dreamville.

Unfortunately, I awoke few hours later to find Charlotte sitting on me and my hands bound above my nude body. I struggled to throw her off me, but found she had also tied my feet to the bed posts as well.

"Charlotte, untie me! Now!"

She moved beside me and began to stroke my chest.

"Charlotte, I'm serious. Untie me now! I will not do this with you."

"Oh, Gordon, you always like to tie me up. I thought I'd try it with you. Be a sport and at least let me try to arouse you."

She had a long peacock feather in her hand and used the large feathered end to brush across my genitals. No matter how I struggled I could feel the light touch of the feather arousing me.

"Stop it!" I was almost yelling now.

She laughed. No matter what I said, my body was reacting differently.

I thought of April, of her gentleness, her tears over Charlotte's appearance and surprisingly it made my erection disappear. I kept saying April's name over and over in my mind, keeping my eyes closed to the creature next to me wielding the feather.

"Gordon, you really don't like this. I'm sorry. Maybe if I leave you like this for a little while you'll be more agreeable. You've never disliked doing this to me. Shouldn't I get to do the same to you?"

"Charlotte, I will never be agreeable to this. I don't love you. I'm in love with April. I want out of this. I want April."

"Who the hell is April? What are you talking about? Is she one of your hallucinations? Oh my god, Gordon, how much do I have to put up with? Is this 'crazy' game you play ever going to end?"

She jumped up in anger, pulled on her robe and went to the door.

"I'll just leave you here for awhile. Maybe your "April" hallucination will have faded by morning."

And there I was, left tied to the bed, nude with only a peacock feather on my genitals. I took a deep breath and closed my eyes again, hoping that I would wake up again soon.

As the morning light began to enter the room and I was still tied to the bedposts, I began to wonder what was real and what was not.

I was schizophrenic. Mad as a hatter. Looney. That was the only thing I did know. For all I knew, April could walk through that door or Charlotte could. Hell, even Mary, Queen of Scots, could for all I knew. I closed my eyes and just hoped it wouldn't be bad.

CHAPTER EIGHT

When the door opened again that morning, it was Charlotte, still in her dressing gown that was open to give me full display of her breasts. She didn't say a word, but just came over to me and removed the feather and began to lightly brush my lower body with her hand.

"Please stop, Charlotte. Untie me. I really must use the restroom. Then I'll be back. I promise." I had to get loose. If that meant promising to have sex with her, then so be it.

She smiled that awful Cheshire cat smile that I now not only loathed, but despised. She untied me and I jumped from the bed as she laid down where I had been previously.

"Secure me first. I want to be ravished when you return," she said.

I walked away to the bathroom without touching her and left her lying there. I was so disgusted with her and myself, especially that I had ever done such things with her in my past.

As I entered the bathroom, I was stunned to find myself fully dressed again and in the lavatory of an airline. I looked about and saw the British Air logo and leaned my forehead against the mirror and sighed with relief. I was back. I hurriedly reopened the door and found that I was back with April in the real world. Dreamville had receded for the time being.

I pushed past the flight attendant and found April still asleep where she had been when I had closed my eyes and I had hallucinated myself into a world with Charlotte. I looked at the face of everyone in First Class to make sure that Will was not there or that I did not smell orange Pekoe tea. I sighed with relief as I stood in the center of the aisle.

"Sir, we'll be landing at Heathrow shortly. Could you please be seated and have your companion prepare for landing?" the flight attendant asked.

"Absolutely. Not a problem."

I said down and gazed at April's peaceful face. I had no idea if my father was correct in his assessment of April's influence over me, but I did know that I only felt love when I looked at her.

I gently shook her shoulder to waken her. She curled closer to me and snuggled against my arm.

"April, dear, we're preparing to land. I'm afraid you're going to have to wake up now. We have a 40 minute layover before the flight to Edinburgh."

She yawned and stretched her arms before rubbing the sleep from her eyes and focusing on my face.

"I'm sorry. How long have I slept?"

"A good part of the flight. You must have been tired."

I tried to take her hand, but she pulled away from me, which surprised me.

"Is something wrong?"

She shook her head and gathered her magazines and put them into her oversized tote bag.

"No, no. Um, how far is Burnock from Edinburgh? Did you arrange transportation or will we have to rent a car?"

She was oddly cool and diffident.

"April, if you don't want to be here, why did you fly across the Atlantic with me? You know I don't need any help."

A glimpse of pain crossed her face and then disappeared into that impassive mask she had been wearing since I first saw her with my father in New York.

"I came because I wanted to. You may not 'need' me, but I thought, well, obviously, I . . . Gordon, do we need to arrange transportation to Burnock once we land in Edinburgh?" She changed the subject very abruptly as if to hide any emotional response she might feel.

As I had started this mess, I could understand that she would be hurt and angry with me, but her indifference surprised me. Rather than respond to it, I acted as if we were merely friends traveling together.

"A car will be waiting to drive us to Burnock. It's about a three hour trip into the highlands. We should arrive by dawn."

She nodded, again indifferent to everything I had just related. I tried to hold my temper and I spent the rest of the journey and the drive to Burnock in silence.

Ferguson, who had worked for the family for years,

had met us at the airport. As he seldom spoke while driving, and April and I said next to nothing to one another, the drive was without a sound except for other traffic and then only the quiet solitude of the drive through the mountains.

It was only when we neared Burnock at dawn that April finally broke her silence as she saw my family home. Burnock was not as large as some estates in the Highlands, but it was large enough for several servants with two wings and a central hall. The grounds were well maintained with a small formal garden, a stable and garage, and the family chapel and churchyard, which had been there almost as long as the house. My ability in business had seen to the continued maintenance of the estate. I might be ill, but my talent at making money seemed to be eerily in balance to my schizophrenia.

"Oh, Gordon, it's lovely. I had no idea it was so beautiful here. Has your family lived here long?"

"Centuries," I replied curtly.

She looked at me with hurt in her eyes and then stared out the window and became quiet again. I hadn't wanted to be short with her, but I didn't want her to stay. No matter how much I had wanted her in Dreamville, I knew that in the real world there was no safe place for her with me. If I had to drive her away from me, so be it. And maybe one day, in the distant future when I was just a memory, she would understand and forgive me.

God only knew if I could forgive myself for what I was trying to do.

CHAPTER NINE

Mrs. MacCurdy, the housekeeper, greeted us and smiled happily as she welcomed April to Burnock.

I cut into her happy little speech and informed her that Ms. Norris would be staying in the blue room in the east wing and asked if she could see to April's things.

Mrs. MacCurdy snapped her mouth shut and tilted her head back at my words.

"Yes, sir. Ms. Norris, if you'll follow me, I'll see you to your room. Mr. Stewart, Mrs. Gregory has prepared a buffet for everyone when they're ready to eat this morning. Oh, and I was told by your father to remind you to telephone your mother."

I nodded and began to walk into the front parlor when I stopped and turned to Mrs. MacCurdy.

"By the way, who else is staying here? I understand

some of the family is to be here."

She smiled slyly. She knew that I was not going to like her response.

"Why your cousins Sheila and her husband, Andrew, Samuel and his missus, Tamara, and Mr. Alex. They're all looking forward to seeing you again and meeting your fiancée, sir, and welcoming her to the family."

I wanted to groan, but tried to remain calm. She had to know the entire situation, but she had just informed me by omission that my cousins had no idea of anything – all which meant that I was actually going to have to treat April appropriately as my fiancée. I sighed and stopped both women on the stairs.

"Since the cousins are here, perhaps you should put Ms. Norris in the yellow room next to mine. I wouldn't want her to be disturbed by them in the east wing."

"As you wish, sir," she said and smiled as she led April to the room next to mine, something she or my parents or even April had possibly been in collusion. With five members of the family in temporary residence and the house staff, I was now in a position I truly dreaded.

What if I began to hallucinate while they were there? What if I hurt April? It kept coming back to that, I thought. Hurting April. How was I going to drive her away with everyone here thinking we were still together?

Good God. I wanted to throttle my father and the lot of them.

I was sitting at the long dining table when Mrs. MacCurdy brought April into the room.

"I'm sure you're hungry, dear. Help yourself to the buffet. Mrs. Gregory made a variety of dishes, including a few American ones for you."

April stared at the massive amount of food before her and she laughed, which puzzled Mrs. MacCurdy.

"Mrs. MacCurdy, she eats oatmeal for breakfast," I said tersely. April's fast friendship with the housekeeper irritated me.

Mrs. MacCurdy sighed and whispered, but still loud enough for my ears.

"tha am fear ag ionnsachadh"

April looked at her in puzzlement.

"It's Gaelic," I said. "And Mrs. MacCurdy could say the same about her own manners."

I heard Mrs. MacCurdy quietly explain to April that the saying loosely translated to "the man had much to learn" as my cousins and their spouses entered the dining hall.

Alex Fletcher, my father's older sister's son, entered first. Dressed immaculately and obviously fresh from a good night's sleep, he greeted April and myself, introducing the rest of the family as he did.

"You must be Miss Pamela Norris! Well, how in the world did my irritable cousin find a beauty such as yourself?"

April blushed and smiled as everyone else greeted her, filled their plates and found seats at the table.

"Please, call me April. It's what my family and Gordon have called me for years."

My cousin Samuel introduced his wife Tamara, who was several months pregnant, and who looked queasily at the food on her plate.

April touched Tamara's hand and replaced Tamara's plate with a small plate with two slices of toast.

"Try some dry toast. It seems to help nausea, at least according to my grandmother."

Tamara smiled gratefully and began to nibble at the toast. Samuel looked at Tamara with relief. Obviously, her morning sickness had been of concern to him, though he had not spoken a word about it to any of us.

Samuel's sister, Sheila and her husband, Andrew, took their seats near me and politely asked about our trip, asking April what she thought of Burnock and Scotland thus far.

"The house is incredible and huge, but I've seen little of the countryside yet. The sun was rising just as we arrived here at the house."

Alex, who had seated himself on the other side of April, placed his hand over hers.

"Since your fiancé is always involved in his business transactions, I'll be more than happy to show you around."

April bowed her head and smiled slightly, but managed to glance my way to gauge my reaction to my cousin's proposal. When I ignored it, she turned back to him.

"That sounds good. Thank you."

"Wonderful!" he said a little too enthusiastically for me. I raised an eyebrow, but said nothing.

"I can certainly see the family resemblance in the four of you, especially your coloring and eyes. If Gordon's father is younger, how is he, um, in "charge" of the family?" April asked.

I quickly responded, wanting to make sure that Alex, and not necessarily April, understood that the order of things had not changed.

"My father is the only son, and by tradition, the one who inherits the estate. He, and then I, and then my descendants, will continue possession of Burnock."

"Alex is older, but the child of my father's eldest sister and is behind my father's family to inherit. Samuel and Sheila are siblings and are the children of Katherine, my younger aunt," I said, pointedly staring at Alex as I spoke.

"Yes, we may look like siblings, but the rule of prima geniture is still in effect, otherwise, the estate would be split into dozens of parcels," Samuel said. "And just as well. Gordon and his father have done more for the family estate than any of us could have. The house is what I believe you Americans would call a "money pit"."

Everyone laughed at Samuel's comment and I realized he was trying to ease the tension Alex had created by his attention to my fiancée.

"Well, Americans rarely follow, what was that? Prime genitor?" April replied.

"Prima geniture," I said correcting her a little too

quickly.

She blushed again, but continued with her statement.

"Yes, well, whatever. We make our own way and certainly don't play "lord of the manner" with the rest of the family. Our family members have equal rights in hereditary matters, no matter their gender."

Alex smirked at her comment.

"Not 'lord', dear. Gordon will be the 'laird'. That's the Scottish term."

"Oh, I thought that was an old word," she said. "I didn't know it was still used."

"Well, it is preferred by some who cling to the old customs," Alex replied, again laughing in my direction.

Everyone at the table became quiet and I noticed that Sheila was staring intently at the white table linens.

"If everyone will excuse me," I said, "I have some business to take care of before it gets too late in New York."

I was across the great hall and in my study before I could hear any more of what they were discussing. I also wanted to be absent from any more talk of my family and their situation. I had enough with which to contend without adding Alex's envy into the mess.

I sat at my desk and stared at the telephone. I knew I should call my parents, but I was angry with my father for inviting Alex. Then I thought that was unfair to my mother and called them, speaking briefly, relating that we had arrived safely and that I would talk with them later. My father tried to interject a question about my health, but I ignored his queries and bid them both good-bye.

I then thought of Rick and how I had left him on his own with the business. I wondered if April had mentioned to him what had happened or that she was coming here with me. Either way, I still needed to telephone him with details on contacting me and any decisions to be made regarding the company.

I also had to apologize for my rudeness in failing to appear for dinner the previous evening. I wondered if he had mentioned anything to April's parents about our absence.

Lisa answered the call and I could hear a television in the background.

"Gordon, is something wrong? You never call so late and we expected to see you and April for supper."

"No, Lisa, forgive me. I forgot about the time. Could I speak with Rick? Is he awake?"

She laughed weakly.

"Not a problem, Gordon. We're still awake."

"Yes, well, good then, that is that I didn't wake you," I replied, but I really didn't want to discuss anything with Lisa. I knew that they had been trying without success to have a child. I really didn't care about such things and had even suggested to April that perhaps they should just hire a surrogate.

When I had told April that they should hire one and that Rick certainly made enough money to do so, I was surprised by her reaction. April had sighed and kissed my cheek. I remembered her saying that I had to know Lisa to understand why that wouldn't happen. It had been the only time we had discussed children and I shook the memory away. The topic of having children was difficult for me to consider and I had often felt that was unfair to April.

"Gordon, it's Rick. Is there a problem?"

"No, Rick, but, well, April and I are in Scotland and may be here for a while. We can conduct any meetings either through the telephone. I'm seeing if I can have a tech crew do some work here so we'll have teleconferencing if needed. I'm leaving you in charge of most decisions for the time being."

"Wait. Did you just say that you and my sister are in Scotland? What the hell happened? We expected you at dinner and you were out of the country? Is April okay?"

I paused. Had April lied? Had she told him? Did he know?

"April is having oatmeal and probably talking with my cousins as we speak. Why would you ask if she's alright?"

"Sorry. My sister can be so contrary and I thought she might have caused some sort of problem for you. You know how stubborn she can be. Truthfully, I'm surprised that she didn't get you to take her to Scotland sooner."

I breathed a sigh of relief. He didn't know and she had kept my secret. He was just being a concerned brother.

"Listen Rick, I'll be in touch with you in a few days. I'm sure you can handle any situations that might arise until then. I'll let you get back to your family. Good evening," I said and hung up before he could say anything else.

Later I would e-mail him from town and give him

specifics for contacting me if I were unavailable except by the house telephone. Mobile service was spotty at Burnock and I knew I would have to resort to installing satellite service in order to conduct business with the New York office if I were to stay at Burnock.

Now that I had finished my calls, I leaned back in the leather chair and propped my feet on the edge of the massive oak desk. I looked out the tall windows and saw the garden glittering with the dew on the spring flowers.

Suddenly April walked into the garden and touched the flowers, bending to smell the blossoms. She had on a summer shirt that was more appropriate to New York summers than a Scottish spring and she suddenly shivered and clasped her arms across her chest, rubbing her bare arms in an attempt to warm them. The sun glowed on her dark curls and I thought once more of how much she looked like she had stepped from a Renaissance painting.

Charlotte had been an English rose, but April was breathtaking in her beauty, with her broad and open smile. How could I let such an angelic creature leave my life?

I stood and started to go to the garden to take her a jacket to warm her when I saw her turn and smile at someone approaching her. Alex. I saw that he was wasting no time in making himself known to her and he removed his sweater and placed it on her shoulders, also placing both his hands on her shoulders and leaving them there as she stood with her back to him and stared out at the vista around the house. I could not hear what they were saying, but I was not going to allow him to charm her the way he had charmed so many women in the past.

They were still standing and talking as I entered the garden.

When Alex saw me, he immediately dropped his hands to his sides.

"Gordon, so glad you've brought this lovely creature to visit here. She is quite humorous in her American way," he said as he shook my hand.

"Be careful. She can be a bit sharp if you criticize her home."

"Oh good Lord, no. I find her a humor a breath of fresh air in this old place. And she was very surprised to find that we have no television here at the house or that her mobile will not work."

"I think she asked us how we could stand living in the 12th century," he said and laughed. "I explained to her that only you lived in the 12th century and that the rest of us lived in Edinburgh and had every modern convenience she could desire."

"How kind of you, Alex," I said drily and looked at April, who had turned her back to both of us.

"I think my fiancée may want to rest after our flight if you don't mind."

April quickly turned at my statement and smiled at Alex.

"I think his 'fiancée' would like to take a walk. Alex, would you mind showing me the grounds? Gordon, you can rest and I'll see you at supper."

"Dinner, my dear. We usually say 'dinner' here. Of course, go with Alex if you like," I said and left the garden as fast as I could. I was furious with her. I was playing my part of the solicitous fiancé. Why wasn't she returning the favor? And my older cousin Alex, who was always prepared to be of assistance to any young lady - what the hell had my father thought in bringing him here?

"Well, he probably thought if she couldn't get the old slap and tickle from you, she might as well enjoy it with him."

Will. Damn it. This was the last thing I needed.

"Will, will you fucking shut up?" I said to him as I opened the door to find the rest of my cousins standing with Mrs. MacCurdy in the great hall.

Sheila rushed over to me and hugged me tightly.

"No one's there, Gordon," she whispered in my ear. "Hold it together for a few, alright?"

"Gordon, we're very pleased that you brought your bride-to-be here to Burnock, though I think Edinburgh might have been a better first stop for her," she said loudly for everyone else to hear.

"So sorry, everyone. The flight was exhausting and I am very jet lagged. It's wonderful to see you," I said, feigning delight at their presence.

After comments on April's friendliness were made and more small talk was completed, Sheila took my arm and led me towards the staircase.

"If everyone doesn't mind, I'm going to escort Gordon upstairs and find out everything I can about his nice fiancée."

Once we had made our way upstairs and were sitting in my room, she immediately became serious.

"Gordon, the others, except probably the staff, do not know that anything is wrong. Your father called me and explained everything to me, but you really must take care and not address your hallucinations in front of the others. You know Alex would jump at the chance to have you declared incompetent in order to lay claim to Burnock."

I sat in the window seat and watched as Alex and April walked across the fields from the house.

"He would do that, wouldn't he? He's always hated my position in the family. Look, Sheila, I did not want April here. I tried to break things off with her. But I don't like the attention Alex is paying her."

She leaned forward in the Queen Anne arm chair next to the fireplace where she sat.

"Why on earth would you want to break off with her? She seems quite nice and appears fascinated by Burnock and Scotland."

I took a deep breath and tried to explain the circumstances to her.

"I, I almost hurt April. I lost control and almost attacked her. I love her too much to put her through bouts of my illness. I wanted her to stay in New York and move on, but there she was with father at the airport and now I'm stuck in a very unpleasant position because the family is here."

"Wait, Gordon, are you saying you love her and that there is no earthly reason not to be with her? Does she love you? I don't understand your reasoning."

"Sheila, did you not hear what I said? I don't want to hurt her. Not emotionally and especially not physically. I'm afraid my delusions and hallucinations might endanger her. Just now one of them was telling me that she was going to have sex with Alex."

"Oh God, Gordon, she's not going to sleep with Alex. He's a leech and I'm sure she saw that the minute she met him. But if she loves you, shouldn't she be allowed to decide whether to marry you?"

I moved over to the bed and sat down on the side of it.

"Sheila, can we talk later? My head is killing me and I really need to get some sleep. I haven't slept since we left New York."

She came over to me and hugged me.

"Get some rest, Gordon. It will be fine. Just don't talk to anyone who's not here, okay?

CHAPTER TEN

It was almost dusk when I awoke and I dressed casually for dinner, hoping that Mrs. MacCurdy and Mrs. Gregory had not made some great production of dinner.

I found everyone in the front parlor waiting for dinner and laughing heartily as April related how I tolerated her 'visits' to her 'Van Gogh' at MoMA.

I sat down next to Sheila and across from April. Alex had ensconced himself on the settee next to her and was sipping wine as she spoke. I watched as his arm was draped behind her on the settee and wondered if he was touching her curls hanging loose behind her.

April still made no eye contact with me and seemed

to engage everyone in the room but me. Mrs. MacCurdy entered and announced that dinner was ready and everyone started to head towards the dining room.

Sheila held my arm for a minute and kept me back from everyone.

"Are you feeling better?"

I nodded and smiled, but never took my eyes off Alex, who was persistent in his attention to April. Dinner was interminably long and afterwards, Tamara, who had revived from her morning sickness, and Samuel insisted on a game of charades. I felt the evening would never end.

I finally excused myself from their company and later heard them making their way upstairs to their bedrooms. I could hear April in the room next to me and I knocked on the door adjoining the yellow room to my bedroom.

She opened it after a few moments and stood blocking my entrance into it.

"Yes?"

"Are you alone?"

"Yes, of course," she said tersely.

"God, April, what the hell is wrong with you? You haven't said ten words to me the entire day and have barely spent any time with me. Is Alex so fascinating that you can't tear yourself away from him?"

"Gordon, don't. Look, I'm tired. If it's alright, I'm going to bed," she said and began to close the door.

I slammed my hand against it and stopped her.

"The hell it is. I want to know what's going on."

I pushed the door open and forced my way into the room.

She stepped back, but she showed no fear as she had the last time I had become so angry with her.

"You can do whatever you want. It's your home, but I am going to bed."

She began to undress and ignored my presence in the room.

"Yes, I can do whatever I want."

I grabbed her shoulders and found myself kissing her.

Instead of pushing me away, she returned my kiss and began to unbutton my shirt. I picked her up and carried her over to the bed and began to undress her as well.

Not a word was spoken, but our eyes never left one another's. I did not tear at her clothing, but removed it gently, restraining myself as best I could. I made love to her slowly and as tenderly as I had ever done and afterward found myself holding her body as close to myself as possible. It had been a perfect time and I was afraid that anything I might say might stop it.

For the first time I found myself unable to speak.

"I love you, Gordon. I'm not leaving you."

She nestled in my arms and fell asleep without another word.

I wanted to scream. What was I going to do? How could I ask her to live this way, never knowing my mood swings, when I would be hallucinating or delusional and in Dreamville? And god forbid, how could we have a family if I were unstable? I would not be the mad father whom everyone excused as simply being "eccentric" as Charlotte had once called it. I would die before I would hurt April or our children.

And the thought of depriving April of a family was devastating. I could not, would not, saddle her with a mad husband and father to her children, no matter how much I wanted to have a family with her.

I slipped from her bed and went back to my own bed. I couldn't find the strength to stay in her arms without thinking of the things that loving me would deny her. I found myself alone and cold as I drifted off to sleep, praying that some solution could be found for this situation that did not break her heart nor leave me alone, miserable, and completely insane.

CHAPTER ELEVEN

I awoke in Dreamville, this time 16 years old and despairing that I had found myself in what I had considered one of the worst times of my life. I was in my American bedroom in Connecticut and it was cold. The room looked nothing like a teenage boy's room. Bare of photos or posters, I had a simple metal bed lamp, school books, and few things I could use to break. Although I was mildly medicated most of the time, I still managed to keep my hallucinations at bay. It would only be many years later when the delusions that always spun around April's life began to increase, the so-called trips to Dreamville that seemed more about her life than mine. In Dreamville, I seemed to be a mere secondary player in the events in her life.

And now that I was here in Dreamville again, I looked out my bedroom and tried to see April's home through the woods beyond our home.

I wondered what she was doing and how I might find a way to talk to her that day at school. School. Oh my god, the thought of it made me ill. I was too tall, too skinny and awkward. If it hadn't been for my friendship with Rick, who had introduced me to basketball, I might not have had any friends at all. And April, she was at that intense stage where she ignored me most of the time.

I remembered her calling our homeroom teacher a "fucking chair Nazi" and grinned. I wondered if this visit was one of those times. One thing I knew about her from the first day I saw her was that she was probably the strongest and most stubborn woman I had ever met. And the most beautiful, even when she was just sixteen and had not begun to blossom into the great beauty she would become.

As I dressed and went downstairs to join my parents, I could hear them quietly talking about me in the dining room.

"But if he's better here, could it be that we're away

from Burnock and not the medications?" my mother asked.

"Claire, you must understand. The medication is what's making it possible for him to have a normal life here. He might have a good, happy life here. And seeing Dr. Fritcher has helped enormously. I think he's going to be better."

I entered the dining room and sat down with them, acting as if I had heard nothing of their conversation.

"Gordon, would you like me to drive you to school?" my mother asked.

I frowned and shook my head.

"Nae, the others will say things."

I looked up at them and was surprised to hear my Scottish burr so pronounced. I knew how to speak without reverting to my old modes of speech. Where had the burr come from?

"Out of your mouth, you idiot."

I looked across from me and saw Will sitting there with his feet propped on the table next to the tureen of oatmeal.

I rolled my eyes. Wasn't Dreamville enough without hallucinations of Will following me? It was going to be a very tough day if he went everywhere I went.

"And I plan on doing just that!"

I noticed something for the first time. Will had an American accent. I tried to remember the first time he appeared when I was living at Burnock and could not recall.

"Of course you can't remember you stupid idiot. It was over 11 years ago. Or was it last year?" he giggled and kicked the table.

"Gordon, don't kick the table," my mother said.

I started to say that it wasn't me, but I knew that would only result in a trip to Dr. Fritcher and I wanted to get to school and find April, even if she ignored me. I just wanted to see her.

"I've got to go. See you after school."

I ran from the house and walked as fast as I could to get to school before April arrived with her brothers, but I was late and found her in the hallway struggling with her locker.

"Motherfucker" she said and dropped her books and papers everywhere.

I stopped and helped her pick them up. Her dark curls were swinging wildly about as a string of expletives were whispered under her breath.

"Let me help you with these to homeroom."

I smiled and held some of the books up.

She raised her eyebrows as if she had never seen me before and grabbed the books from my hands.

"Not in this life," she said and turned back to the locker, ignoring me.

This visit was slightly different from the other times and became markedly strange when Will leaned against the locker next to her and began to make faces at her.

"She is one skinny bitch now, no matter how she looks later. I think I like Charlotte more. I think you did, too."

"I did not," I said.

April turned to me. "What? Did you say something?"

"No, see you in class," I said and stomped off towards my homeroom. Will was still standing next to her and flipped her books from her arms again. She cursed again and began to pick her things up again.

What the hell? He was my hallucination. How could he touch her books? This made no sense. I became afraid and froze in the hall, watching her as Will stood over her laughing.

I didn't know what to think of this. I had always called Dreamville what April had called it because she said it didn't sound like a hallucination since I never showed manifestations of it the way I had when Will appeared in my real life.

In my real life, the few times Will had appeared had resulted in conversations and arguments with thin air. April would get me to Dr. Fritcher and it usually helped. Then I remembered the orange pekoe tea he always offered me. That tea was another sign of a delusion. So why was there tea in his office?

I went into homeroom and sat down, knowing April would be behind me any second. Suddenly the doorknob was turning and it was as if the door refused to open. It opened slightly and then slammed shut. Finally it opened and April stumbled in, tripped, dropped her books again and said "Shit" loudly.

"Pamela Norris!"

Mrs. Brown was upset with April and told her to sit. April's face was bright red and she apologized and hurried to her seat. I looked to the door and saw Will standing just outside, waving wildly at me and laughing at April. Had he caused April's problems?

Nothing seemed real. This, as in my other visit to Dreamville, was unlike any delusion I had experienced. I glanced over at April and saw that she was almost in tears. I scowled at Will and then ignored him. Maybe if I ignored him, she would be alright, though I still didn't understand how my hallucination could interact with other people and I started thinking about that tea again.

I was starting to think that I was truly coming undone in this delusion. First the incident at the apartment, then the plane and the visit to London with Charlotte, Will antagonizing me at Burnock in the real world and now this visit to Dreamville where he was antagonizing April. It made no sense.

I went through the day on autopilot for the most part as I did most times I was in Dreamville, but today I watched April throughout the day to make sure that Will did not appear around her again. It was then that I had a horrible thought. Could Will harm April in the real world the way he did in my delusions? Was she any safer with or without me?

I sought out Rick and bummed a ride home with him. April, who was driving, was none too happy with my presence in the car, but was very quiet as she drove to her home.

Rick invited me in and she disappeared somewhere in the house while we sat in the family room and played video games. I was just about to head home through the woods when we heard April scream like a banshee somewhere in the house.

Rick and his brothers Carl and David ran up the stairs followed by me. Rick slung open the door and looked for his sister who he discovered was cowering in the far corner of the room.

"Shit, April, what the hell?"

She was shaking visibly.

"There . . . there was someone standing there," she said, her voice trembling.

For some reason Rick didn't tease her or make her feel worse. He went to her and led her from the room and down the stairs.

"Hey, Gordon, check that door to the third floor and see if it's locked," he called out from the landing.

Something about this was both familiar and wrong. I suddenly remembered the dream where I had dragged April up those steps, raped her and held a gun to her chest. I shivered and started down the steps behind April and her brothers only to be stopped by Will.

"Starting to see the bigger picture, now?" he laughed and vanished.

CHAPTER TWELVE

I awoke in a cold sweat and jumped from the bed to go into the yellow room where I had left April. She was gone and the bed was made.

I went back into my room and ran my hand across my head. I could hear voices outside and I went to the window to see April and the rest of my family in the garden having breakfast. The sun was bright and the day looked much warmer than it had the day before.

And again, there was Alex sitting as close to April as possible, but behind her I saw Will standing and I threw on a pair of jeans and an old Green Day t-shirt and ran down to where they were.

"He's alive," Alex said, trying to do a Dr. Frankenstein imitation.

April looked up at me and smiled broadly, enough

for Alex to see that he had just lost one battle in the war for her attention.

"And barefoot," Samuel said. "Definitely spent too much time in America."

April stood and slid an empty chair next to her for me and I sat down next to her, looking up to see if Will was still standing about anywhere. Both April and Sheila noticed it and together began to talk to me about getting out today and driving into the village.

"Yes, Gordon, why not take April into the village and show her around? You certainly don't want to spend your vacation here with us always around."

Alex looked unhappy at being excluded from our excursion and miserable when April leaned over to kiss me.

"April, I wanted to thank you for telling me about the dry toast. It's helped a great deal," Tamara said.

"Well, I hope I don't have it," April replied.

Alex looked aghast.

"You're not . . ."

"Of course not. I meant when I do, or if I do."

He sighed loudly in relief and although I was none too happy with his response, I felt the same way myself. I became terrified that she was pregnant or might become pregnant. We had not used contraception in the last few weeks and it was possible. Good god, what would I do then?

I put my arm around her shoulder and whispered in her ear that perhaps we should go ahead and drive into town before Alex ended up in the back seat.

She laughed, kissed me again and excused herself from the table. The rest of the family followed her into the house except for Alex.

"Still drinking American coffee, I see."

I nodded, not wanting to talk to him lest he somehow try to invite himself on our trip.

"Why don't you just stay there permanently if you like it so much?"

"Because, Alex, this is my home and will be until I die when it becomes my children's home."

He snorted and stalked off into the house.

I suddenly felt a cool breeze against my arms and my feet were beginning to get cold. I gulped down the rest of my coffee and took off upstairs to dress.

As I entered my bedroom I saw that the door between April's room and mine was closed. I opened it and stared in horror as I saw Will lounging on the bed, watching April as she undressed.

"Get the hell out of here!" I exclaimed before I could think.

April looked at me and then around the room.

"Is he here?"

I closed my eyes, swallowed my shame, and nodded.

She came to me and put her hands on my shoulders.

"Gordon. Gordon. Open your eyes and look at me. Look at my face. He's not real. It's okay. We're alone."

I started to turn my head back to the bed, but she held her hand to my stubbled cheek and stopped me.

"No. Don't look. He's not there. Kiss me and go get dressed," she added.

I lowered my head in shame.

"I'm so sorry. You shouldn't have to go through this. You're too precious to me. I'm sorry."

"Stop it. Go get dressed and have a shave. We're going to have a lovely day," she smiled.

I returned her smile and went back to dress for the trip to the village. She was right. It was going to be okay. And I was going to buy condoms to make sure.

The drive into the village was not far, but the small,

winding roads took concentration and I wanted to talk to April. I hated to ruin her happy mood, but the delusions, the visits to Dreamville, were beginning to concern me. I needed to know that she would be safe if I did drive her to leave me, which of course I did not want to tell her. I actually did not want to see her leave my life.

"You're quiet."

She held her hand out the open window and let it wave in the air.

"I'm happy. I'm with you. I'm also astonished that you would ever want to leave Scotland. It's very beautiful here."

I took a deep breath as we left the estate grounds and entered the main road.

"April, I've had more than a few hallucinations and visits to your 'Dreamville' in the past week."

She turned to the right in the seat to face me. I saw the concern and quickly returned my visual focus to the road ahead.

"Why didn't you tell me? What were they?"

"The hallucinations were almost all of Will."

"Like this morning?"

I nodded as I kept the Astin Martin close to the

mountain side. I did little driving in America, but at Burnock, I drove everywhere and so remembering on which side of the road to remain was never too difficult.

"What about Dreamville? What delusions?"

I decided that mentioning the one containing my time with Charlotte was not a wise thing to do. I decided instead to mention the one where we were sixteen. I told her about it and described how Will had appeared in it and had kept bothering her.

"Wait a minute. Gordon, that wasn't a delusion or Dreamville. That was a memory. I distinctly remember that day because that was the day I . . . well, I probably should have told you, but I was really terrified because I did see someone in my bedroom."

"I had been afraid of the third floor of the house for years. My brothers were as well. My parents and grandmother always dismissed it, but we seldom went up there. I'm convinced that my father put the lock on that door for a reason other than keeping the heating bills down."

"A memory?"

"It has to be. Everything you just said happened exactly as you described it, except for my seeing 'Will'," she said.

I shifted gears as we rolled into town and slowed down.

"Could I have mixed Will into a memory of you?"

She shrugged and looked out the window.

"I don't know. I just know someone was in my bedroom and that I kept having trouble holding anything that day. By the time I drove home I was in a very bad mood."

I pulled the Astin Martin in front of one of the shops and parked. I could not let this go before we went walking down the streets.

"Are you absolutely sure, April? This worries me a great deal. Am I confusing memories, hallucinations and Dreamville delusions together? If I am, I could be getting much worse."

She had removed her safety belt and leaned over to where I sat.

"Why does a memory have to be something from Dreamville? Did this happen last night? It could be a dream, just as the nightmare was last week."

I shook my head.

"It was after I had gone back to my room last night,

but it felt like a delusion, not a dream or a memory."

I pounded my fist against the steering wheel in frustration. I was losing the ability to distinguish between reality and the products of my schizophrenia.

"Gordon, stop. There has to be a logical answer. Show me your hometown. Introduce me to the people you knew when you were young. Forget about the rest of it for now."

I leaned to kiss her and smiled. I had never believed I could have her love me and here she was, urging me away from the darkness and to the light. Just as I was about to tell her how much I loved her, I watched as she slid out of the car and closed the door, staring around the village as if trying to decide where to go first. I exited the car and joined her on the sidewalk where she took my hand in hers.

"There," she said and pointed towards a fabric shop across the street."

"Fabric? But you don't sew."

She laughed as she pulled me into the store.

"But I want to see your family tartan and buy some authentic, Scottish wool for home. I can think of several different uses for it."

"Maybe even for a kilt for you," she whispered and giggled.

"I already have several," I said and sighed. There was no stopping her. When she discovered that there were several variations of the Stewart tartan, she had amassed almost three large parcels with more wool than anyone could use. She left a very happy merchant who had taken her natural and open American friendliness to heart.

We visited several shops before I found myself laden with more bags and parcels than I could manage. The one place I had not managed to visit was the apothecary and I wanted to go there alone. I had determined that if we found ourselves making love again that I would be prepared. I would face the discussion of no children then. She was so happy that I felt I could not broach it now without making her sad.

"I'm going to take these things and put them in the boot and I'll meet you at the pub down the street."

She waved as she walked down the street and I walked back across to the Astin Martin, put the parcels inside it, and then went into the apothecary to procure the condoms.

Ten minutes later I entered the pub to find that she

had already managed to make friends with the owners and the regulars at the bar. I walked up to her and put my hand at the small of her back.

"Oh, Gordon. They have haggis. I want to try some. I've always heard about it, but never thought I would actually get to try real Scottish haggis."

The others around us laughed, but with her and not at her.

"My darlin', I think you might want something else. Why not some lamb stew?"

The owner leaned in and said, "Young Mr. Stewart's probably right. It's on the menu for tourists, mostly. The lamb will be much better."

She wrinkled her nose unhappily.

"Well, if you say so. But I want your best Scotch with the lamb."

I ordered the stew as well, but abstained from the Scotch as I had the drive back.

We left town a few hours later, leaving a village with happy merchants who had taken to my fiancée with a friendliness I seldom saw offered to tourists or even visitors from the cities. I knew how they felt. It was a love-hate relationship for them. They needed the tourists to maintain their businesses, but they disliked the comments and condescension that was either intentionally or unintentionally aimed at them. And being the next 'Laird', I had been of the receiving end of that same treatment, too.

As we drove back, April chatted on about how she adored my home, the Scotch having loosened her personality quite a bit. She did not notice that I barely spoke as we returned to Burnock.

When we arrived at the house, the strong Scotch in the middle of the day turned on her and she became queasy. I half carried her upstairs to her room where I laid her on her bed and helped her to undress. She had barely removed her jeans when the nausea drove her to the bathroom. I could hear her being ill and sat on her bed for a few moments before I joined her, holding her dark hair back and helping her as the contents of her stomach emptied.

Her physical symptoms finally stopped and I wet a wash cloth to help her clean up. I ran a bath as she cleaned her face with the cloth and then helped her to finish undressing before lifting her into the warm bath.

I sat in the floor next to her, her fingers clasping

mine as she closed her eyes and allowed the water to relax her body. When I noticed that she had fallen asleep in the tub, I lifted her from the water with a bath sheet and carried her back to her bed. She hardly stirred as I sat down on the bed next to her.

I found the episode strange as I had seen her drink much more at other times and she had never had this reaction. I kissed her forehead and left her there to sleep off the scotch.

"She's going to have a real headache later," Will said from the fireside chair as I entered my bedroom. Again, I ignored him and opened my night table drawer to put the condoms I had purchased.

"Too late for those, you idiot!" he called out.

I whirled around to face him and saw nothing but the empty chair. I sat down and stared at the condoms I was still holding. I closed my eyes and prayed that he was wrong, that the hallucination was just a manifestation of my own fears. I shoved the boxes in the drawer and slammed it shut.

Before I went downstairs, I looked through the doorway at April's sleeping body. As much as I wanted children with her, I could not doom one of them to my madness. It was a curse I would wish on no one.

As I went into the parlor, I found Alex sitting alone, puffing on a pipe.

"Put that damn thing out. There's no smoking in the house and you might think of Tamara's health before you do something so stupid."

"Excuse me, 'Laird' Gordon," he said sarcastically and emptied the pipe into an ashtray next to where he sat.

"Alex, don't be an ass. Why are you here? I hardly think my father invited you."

"This is my family home as well, Gordon. Do not forget that. Should you not inherit, I will. And, as you've had some problems of late, I can see that possibility becoming more of a reality."

I stared at him in anger. How had he discovered what was going on or was he just guessing?

"And what problems would those be, Alex? Ones that you hope for?"

He stood next to me and looked up at me. I had never realized what a little bastard he was.

"Well, we'll see how things go, won't we? You can't hide in America forever," he said and left the room just as Sheila entered.

She stared at him in puzzlement and then looked to me.

"Gordon, you look as if you've seen a ghost! What just happened?"

"I'm not sure. He wants me to think he knows something, but I think he's bluffing. Not unless someone has told him something."

"Gordon, he knows nothing. He's a petulant and greedy ass. I don't know why in heaven's name you invited him here."

"I didn't. Did you or Samuel tell him you were coming up for the week?"

"Lord, no. Andrew can't stand him and Samuel never talks to him. Did your father invite him?"

"I don't think so. I made mention of something to that effect and he didn't react. No, someone here at the house must have told him, though I can't think of whom. He's rude to everyone on staff."

I walked over to the long windows and looked out at the higher mountains in the distance. Fog was beginning to descend. We would have rain tomorrow and that meant being stuck in the house with everyone. Not a pleasant prospect.

"Where is April?"

I walked back to the sofa and sat down next to Sheila.

"Sleeping off a bit of a bottle of Scotch, lamb stew, and a shopping trip to the village," I laughed.

"I think she bought something from every shop in town and then wanted to eat haggis at the pub."

"Well, they must have loved her, then. Gordon, she is so nice and so kind. A truly good spirit. And she's good for you. I can see it when you're not snapping at everyone."

I sank into the sofa and looked up at the ceiling

"There's plaster trim that's missing from the ceiling," I said feeling no desire to continue the conversation's direction toward my illness.

Sheila looked up and then at me.

"Don't be trying to change the subject, Gordon. We can talk about the ceiling later."

"No, you're right. I was in a bad state when we arrived and delusional. But today has been good and you're right about April. I'm just afraid I'm not good for her."

"Nonsense. She's very happy with you. Do you think

she'll be joining us for dinner?"

I laughed at that question.

"Nae, she will most likely sleep till morning. She seemed to have a very strong reaction to the Scotch and the lamb stew."

Sheila looked down at her hands and then focused her blue eyes on my face.

"Gordon, could she be, well, could she be pregnant? Unless she drank half the bottle of Scotch, that's an awfully strong reaction."

I wiped my hand across my face.

"God, I hope not. It's not impossible, but it's unlikely."

Shelia patted my knee and took my hand.

"Then no need to borrow trouble. Come, let's join the others in the dining room. Your talk of lamb stew has made me hungry."

I followed her lead and felt at peace until I realized that she had echoed April's words in New York about borrowing trouble. Something suddenly felt very, very wrong.

CHAPTER THIRTEEN

"Did you eat?"

I heard April's soft voice through the open door after I had finished dinner and had sat with my family, talking about the estate, how we should see one another more, how the business was doing – everything but April, although Alex did attempt a few jabs at me over her absence.

I had just walked into my bedroom when I heard her voice from the yellow room. I went in and sat on the bed next to her.

"Yes, love. Did you sleep? Are you feeling better? Do you need something?"

She shook her head and reached out for me. I stretched out on the bed next to her, the bedding a barrier between her nakedness and my growing desire for her. We began by just touching one another's faces and kissing gently. Our kisses became more intense and I felt the pull of our bodies moving closer one another.

"April, are you sure you feel alright?"

"I feel fine, though I'm embarrassed that I had a bit too much to drink."

I undressed quickly and was just about to slip under the sheets with her when I remembered the condoms.

"Don't move," I said.

I grabbed one of the foil packages and jumped back in bed with her.

"What have you got?"

I paused, afraid of how she would react.

"A condom. I bought them at the apothecary in the village. I didn't bring any from New York."

"Well, hurry up, and open that thing. I want you in me now."

"Yes, my dear," I grinned and started to unroll the condom on my penis when the condom broke.

"Damn!"

I ran and retrieved another one and the same thing happened again.

"Did you buy the wrong size," she said, laughing at my frustration.

"Oh, to hell with it. Come to me. I'll pull out."

I climbed over her and slid into her effortlessly. I could feel the heat from inside her around me as I began to move in and out. She wrapped her legs around my lower back and lifted herself to meet me with every thrust. I knew that I could be making a mistake, but I could not stop.

Afterward, when we both lay apart and the sheets were damp with sweat, she kissed me and laughed.

"You know what they call 'pulling out' back home, don't you?"

I grimaced but said nothing.

"They call it useless."

"April, we really should have been thinking of birth control the last year. We've taken a lot of chances."

"I know," she said and curled next to me, pulling the coverlet around us, which I pushed away in frustration. Why could I not get her to understand my concerns about children?

"We've never talked very much about having children. April, do you want children? What if my illness affects them if we have them? I just don't think I could put this burden on someone else, especially a child of ours."

She was silent and I could see her face as she was considering my words.

"Gordon, I want children with you and I think you worry too much about what might happen. It's just that you obsess over the future so much that you forget the present. Either way, I'm fairly certain we have nothing to worry about right now."

I sat up in frustration and stared down at her. Her dark curls spread out across the pillow and I could not help but touch them, twisting my finger in one and feeling the soft silkiness of it.

"You make me crazy. Why can't you understand my feelings on this?" I asked.

"Oh, I understand you. Just as I did when you threw me out of our home. Just as you ignored me on the plane and here the first day after we arrived. It's all fear. You can't live in fear, Gordon, or you won't have a life."

I thought about what she had said and she was right

that I should not have forced her to leave our home. I should have left. Then she might not have known that I had gone to Scotland, although knowing her determination she would have eventually found me.

And my weakness in giving in to our mutual sexual desires only reinforced the strength of our relationship. I had come here with every intention of driving her away and here I was in bed discussing children and having sex without birth control. What a fool I was.

I stayed in her bed that night and I slept in her arms, without dreams, without nightmares. I stopped thinking about the problems and let myself drift off. I would think about our situation tomorrow.

I was surprised to find her still next to me in the morning. She was an early riser and often was up and about several hours before me. I opened my eyes to find her lying on her side, her head propped on one hand as she watched me.

"Was I snoring? Sorry if I woke you."

She leaned in and kissed me softly.

"No, I was just thinking of us, of you, of what I could do to make you see how much I need you."

I rolled over and sat up on the side of her bed,

grabbing my trousers from the floor and putting them on.

"Gordon, why do you do that? Every time I want to talk, I end up seeing your back as you walk away."

"Dear, it's late. We need to go downstairs and have breakfast. The rest of the family will already be down there."

She jumped up on the bed into a sitting position with her legs tucked under herself. The coverlet had fallen away and the only thing covering her body was the almost waist length dark curls of her unbound hair. I made the mistake of turning to speak to her as she sat up. I held my breath for a second and placed my right hand on the door facing. God help me, I wanted to get back in that bed with her more than I wanted anything else at that moment.

"Damn it, Gordon! Who cares? We're on vacation as far as they're concerned and we're going to be married. You don't seriously think that they think we're not sharing a bed, do you?"

I pushed myself away from the doorway and into my room. I could not look at her. It was far too difficult.

"Just get dressed or don't. I'm going down for breakfast," I said and shut the door, leaving her still sitting and waiting for me to return.

I took a quick shower, dressed and was astonished to find myself alone in dining hall. It seemed that I had overestimated the time and that I was actually much earlier for breakfast than I had thought. I filled my plate from the sideboard and sat down, deciding to come up with a plan of some sort to keep myself away from April. I knew that as long as I responded to her with love, desire, or kindness that she would continue to stay and that sooner or later I would give in again. I had to be hard on myself and her, no matter how much it hurt either of us.

She followed me into the dining hall about five minutes after I had finished eating. I had the morning newspaper and held it up to my face so that I might be able to keep her from engaging me in conversation. I was wrong in that assumption. She said nothing. She filled her plate and sat at the farthest place setting from me. I glanced at her and felt myself stiffen at the sight of her. Not that she was dressed in anything more provocative than a pair of Levis and a cotton blouse, she just had that effect on me, especially when she ignored me. A hold-over I supposed from when we were in school when I had loved her from what seemed like miles away.

We were still sitting in silence as the rest of the family made their way to breakfast. Sheila, who entered first, raised her eyebrows at me at the distance between April and myself. Alex, however, had no such problems and quickly seated himself next to April.

"Lovely April, how are you this fine morning?"

Her face lit up as she smiled at him and I could feel my lip curling slightly. I raised the paper higher to hide my face from them. If I were going to be cold, I could not allow her to see my jealousy and jealousy it was. Right then I wanted to jump across the table and pound my fist into Alex's smug face.

"Alex, are there horses here on the estate? I'd love to go riding if you have time to join me."

Alex raised his eyebrows this time, surprised at April's request.

"We have horses, but Alex isn't much for them," Samuel said before Alex could speak. "Gordon is the true equestrian in the family."

"Untrue, Samuel. Ms. Norris, I would be happy to join you."

I kept my face buried in the newspaper as the

conversation continued, but I could feel my face burning with anger at the discussion and the thought of April spending the day with Alex.

"Excellent. Can we go after breakfast?" April replied to Alex.

Without a word, I put the paper down and rose to leave the room. I could see anger in April's eyes, no matter how she smiled for Alex. I turned my back before she could clearly see my own anger and made my way to my study.

The damn bastard. How dare he take my fiancée riding on my horses? I started to throw a small bronze horse paperweight across the room when I stopped myself.

Why was I so angry? Wasn't this what I wanted? For her to want to leave me or a legitimate reason for me to break off the engagement? I took a deep breath, sat down at the desk and absentmindedly transferred the paperweight from one hand to the other, the whole time trying not to think of Alex touching her. Of anyone touching her. I realized I was obsessing over her with anyone and for the first time felt the jealousy turning dark.

Had Sheila not come into the study, I would have continued with those thoughts and when I saw the concern on her face, I felt fear - not that I was losing control, but that I had lost it altogether.

"Gordon, are you a complete idiot? What were you thinking? Why didn't you speak up? Even Samuel found the riding trip distasteful and certainly inappropriate behavior."

I shook my head and put the paper weight back down on the desk.

"She's American, Sheila. Our family protocol is different than what she is used to. Don't blame her. She's angry with me, anyway."

"Truly, Gordon, I'm not enjoying this and I know Andrew would rather be back in Edinburgh than watching this ghastly melodrama play itself out."

I smiled and held my hand out towards the door.

"Sheila, there's no reason for you and Andrew to stay the week. You should go back home. I'm sure you miss your friends and your children. I'm going to be preoccupied with having satellite internet and telephone service installed as well as working each day. I really don't have time to entertain anyone."

"Gordon, if you allow this to continue, you'll regret it and Alex will have both your fiancée and your title. And God help us all if that happens. He'll waste every penny you've made after he's had you declared mentally incompetent."

"Oh, and if he takes April, you'll still have to see her – with him! Is that what you want? Really?"

I leaned forward with my arms against the desk, my hands clasped tightly, and lowered my eyes.

"If it keeps her safe and makes her happy. I'm fearful that I will hurt her one day and that I could not live with."

"But," I continued, "I seriously doubt that she will become enamored by Alex. I'd rather she went back to New York and found someone far, far away from me, someone who deserves her."

Sheila stood up and threw a sheaf of papers at me.

"Oh, you fool! You stupid fool! She's not going to give up and run home. She might take Alex on just so she could be close to you!"

I had not considered that possibility. I had thought a simple plan the best. Drive her away with a distant and cold demeanor. Make her hate me and everything around me. I never thought that she might actually marry Alex just to be near me. And Alex, Alex would not make her happy. I knew that. He could not be faithful to any woman.

"Oh my God, Sheila, she has to go home. I cannot live this way. It's tearing me apart. She must go."

"Well, now you're finally seeing the light."

I looked to the corner and saw Will standing there, his arms folded across a white and navy tennis sweater.

"Go to hell."

Sheila was completely taken aback.

"Did you just tell me to . . ." she said and then looked in the direction I was staring.

"Gordon, there's no one there. Who do you see?"

I rubbed my eyes and Will had vanished.

"I'm sorry, Sheila. This is why I need her to leave. God only knows what I might do or say if I become so deluded that I become paranoid."

"I think that the only times I've seen you have these delusions are when you're afraid of losing her. She might be the one keeping you rooted in reality."

She turned and went to the door.

"Andrew and I will stay through Friday and then

you're on your own. But I implore you, Gordon, do not drive her into Alex's arms. Get him out of here before we leave. Maybe then you can solve this equation of balancing your illness and your love for her."

I walked over to the window after she exited the study and stared beyond the garden to the far pasture where I could see two small figures on horseback fading into the distance. I was unaware that I had once more picked up the paperweight and this time I did throw it, watching it fly through one of the small window panes and disappear somewhere in the garden.

CHAPTER FOURTEEN

By noon I had made all the arrangements for the satellite crew to come up the next day to install the electronics for the internet, television and telephone. I had to pay a substantial fee to get them to drive from Edinburgh to Burnock the next day, but I had to get back to work as soon as possible. I could not face another empty day in that study, thinking of where or what April and Alex might be about.

It also gave me a reason to expel my houseguests. I would ask their pardon that I needed to work and that as April's brother was my vice president, that I would need her assistance with getting the office in working order. I really didn't mind Shelia and Samuel being at the estate, but I had to rid the place of Alex. He was like vermin that kept nibbling away at my piece of mind.

I heard April and Alex's voices from the great hall when they returned from their ride. Alex was rather aggressively pursuing the possibility of a trip to the pub with April, but she pled exhaustion and urged him to drive into the village himself. I heard him extract a promise for a trip the next day and then heard his car heading away from the house.

I wanted to go into the great hall and greet April, but I quietly closed the door and sat to work at my desk. Seeing her would make me want her now and I knew that would only encourage her.

As I began to concentrate on my work again, I felt the room shift slightly and could smell the strong scent of orange pekoe tea mixed with Charlotte's perfume. I looked up to find her leaning over my shoulder, her ample bosom barely restrained by the low cut and tissue thin red tunic she was wearing. I sighed and closed my eyes, praying that she would disappear. I opened them to find her unfortunately still there, but now sitting on the edge of my desk, almost in my lap.

"Hello, lover. Why not stop this boring work and let me give you a little treat for an afternoon break?"

Oh, God, I was at Burnock with Charlotte. What the hell was happening? She had never come to Burnock. Too rural and too far from London for her.

"Charlotte, when did you get here? I've got to work. I can't entertain you right now."

"Well, now some real fun!" I heard Will speak from the corner he had previously vanished. "Give her a good spanking and then take her across that big desk."

"Oh for God's sake, will you leave me alone!"

Charlotte wrapped her arms around me, my face so close to her bosom that I could almost taste her perfumed skin. She straddled my lap and began to undo my belt and unzip my trousers. I tried to push her away from me, but there was little room between myself and the desk with her on my lap.

She slid her hand into my trousers and I grabbed it and then the other one and finally extricated myself from her.

"Charlotte, for God's sake, please leave!"

"Oh lover, not until you give me what I can see you want by the bulge in your pants."

I shoved her away from me and watched in horror as she fell through the window. I hadn't meant to push her that hard. In fact, I was sure I hadn't. I turned to see Will standing next to me and realized that he had shoved her as well. Now she was lying halfway through the window with her head at an odd angle and a large shard of glass embedded in her neck.

Suddenly, the door to the study flew open and April came running through, followed by Sheila.

"I don't know what happened. She wouldn't leave me alone. I shoved her, but she must have tripped. Is she alright?"

April and Sheila just stared at me.

"Well, for God's sake, call and get an ambulance!

"Gordon," Sheila said, "Who are you talking about? There's no one there."

"Hell, Sheila, she's right there. It's Charlotte. When did she get here? How did she know I was here?"

"Oh, Gordon, she's not here," Sheila spoke quietly. "There is no Charlotte. There never has been."

I stared at her, terrified at her words. April was silent throughout, her face anguished and tears falling down her face.

"You see her, don't you, April? Please tell me you do."

April shook her head and lowered it as she moved to me and quietly zipped my trousers and fastened my belt. I watched her hands as they worked and saw that the tears continued to fall as she did. As I collapsed back into the chair, I glanced over to the window and could still see Charlotte's broken body lying half in and half out of the window while Will stood in the corner and laughed.

"We heard you yelling and came quickly. We thought you might have hurt yourself."

Sheila came around to where I sat and helped me to my feet.

"Come, Gordon, let's go upstairs before Alex returns from the pub. We can't have him see you this way."

"No, wait, what do you mean there never has been a Charlotte? I know there was. I was engaged to her. She was not a delusion as Will is."

April came to my side and took my hand.

"Sheila just told me about Charlotte, about your breakdown three years ago. I'm sorry, Gordon. I thought she was real, too."

"No," I said quietly, trying to grasp what was real and what was not.

"I must truly be unhinged. How could I have

continued to think that seeing Charlotte were just delusions fueled by a past relationship."

I dropped April's hand and allowed Sheila to lead me from the room as Will continued to laugh from his corner. I looked back into the room as April knelt and began to pick up small pieces of glass from where I had thrown the paperweight. I watched as her hands passed through Charlotte's body and chills ran up my spine.

"Leave it, April," Sheila said. "Gordon needs you now. I'll see to the broken pane later."

As we went into my bedroom, I could see the door into the yellow room was tightly closed. I could barely hear sobs from the other side of the door and wondered who was weeping, but was so confused that I did not mention it, thinking it was a hallucination. Sheila led me to the chair and sat on the end of the bed while April went to retrieve my medication.

"Sheila, I can't believe that there never has been a Charlotte."

She wiped her eyes and took my hands in hers.

"Gordon, Charlotte was a hallucination you had in London. She does not and never has existed."

"But we were engaged. She broke things off when I

told her of my illness. She has to exist. I have very specific memories of her, of her home in Kensington."

April handed me the pills and a glass of water. She wandered over to the window seat and sat down, watching the road and listening as Sheila and I talked. As Sheila recounted my stay in London after finishing school in America, she told me that my memories of that time were probably buried by the intensive methods used to bring me back from the abyss.

"I think you created Charlotte as a defense mechanism against whatever had caused the break and the pain of the treatments. Your father wanted to bring you back to the United States, but the doctors here said that it was not possible at the time."

"After you started to come back from wherever you had gone that year, you were brought here to Burnock to recuperate and regain control again. The house in Kensington has been shuttered for years. It was your house, Gordon. You lived there alone. I know because I visited you there. I . . . I was the one who found you," she continued.

I could see April surreptitiously wiping tears off her cheek as she continued to watch the road. I shielded my own eyes with my hand. I could not bear to look at either April or Sheila.

"Samuel and I were told of your illness by Mother when we were younger, but she made us both swear to never mention it to Alex or his family. She was as worried as your parents were that he would use it to take the land and title."

"Of course, that was not a problem. Neither of us has ever been able to stand Alex. But someone had to tell him about this week and it had to be someone on the staff. I cannot believe that my brother would tell him."

She stood and walked over to where April sat and looked out the window as they both saw Alex's car making its way around the pastures on the gravel drive to the house.

"We need to find out who is giving him information. Thank heavens no one but April and I are aware of what happened today."

She placed her hand on April's shoulder and smiled.

"I'll leave him to you and make excuses for your absence from dinner. You know, 'soon to be married' sort of things. No one will question it. I'll bring a tray up later for both of you myself if you want."

Shelia left the room and April continued to sit at the window as dusk was beginning to fall.

"I'm sorry, April. I thought Charlotte was real. I have so many memories of her, not to mention the nightmares and delusions, visits to Dreamville that involved her."

April moved from the window seat and sat at my feet, lying her head on my lap. I brushed her hair from her damp cheek with my hand and she took it in her own hands and gently kissed it.

"I can't believe I've been jealous of Charlotte for the past year," she said and wryly smiled. "I didn't think I could ever live up to her wit or beauty or sophistication. She seemed to be everything I wasn't."

I lifted her head up to face her.

"Good god, I never wanted you to feel that way. I've loved you since I first saw you in Connecticut. I never compared your beauty or love with her."

"But April, what happened today should tell you how dangerous being with me can be. You cannot take a chance on my hurting you because I think you're someone else or if I hallucinated that you were unfaithful and hurt you or worse . . ."

"Can Alex really take everything from you?" she

149

asked, ignoring my litany of concerns.

"Yes," I sighed, "But that's not the point. You are in danger staying with me. That's why I've been trying to push you away."

She stood and looked down at me.

"It explains why Alex has done nothing but interrogate me about you, our relationship, and your business. Except when he wasn't trying to 'charm' me. And he's so slimy and so obvious."

"I only went riding with him to make you jealous. And, well, I was ticked off at you for acting so cold this morning. I thought if I made you jealous, you might fight back for me."

She sat on the edge of bed and looked at me.

"Now I think that trying to make you jealous was a bad idea. If Sheila is right, then the delusions are being borne of some sort of insecurity about me."

I shook my head.

"No, I wish it were that simple. Then I could just toss out Alex and be with you. But even if it were that, I couldn't lock you away from the rest of the world with me. That's not fair to you."

She pursed her lips and then laid back against the

bed.

"Then tell me the rest. Tell me everything."

I walked over and laid next to her on the bed.

"I can't tell you that. It's too disgusting, too horrible. I thought my relationship with Charlotte was dark and I was ashamed of it. Now that I know it never happened, I have to wonder where those thoughts, those desires, where did they come from?"

"Gordon. I'm never going to leave you. I'm never going to love anyone the way I love you. I'd rather spend the rest of my life alone than live without you."

"You can be cold and cynical. You can push me away. You can be mean to me. But I'll always be there. I'll go wherever you go. I will never stop loving you. Ever. You are the love of my life."

I pulled her over to me and held her close.

"If I truly loved you the way you say you love me, I would never allow you to make such a sacrifice. That's what I should do. It's what I've been trying to do – push you away from me. But I've been weak and I've always fallen back into your arms.

She laid her hand upon my chest over my heart.

"If you truly love me, then you should want me to be

happy and I will never be happy without you."

She snuggled closer to me as the stress of the afternoon overcame both of us. We fell asleep in one another's arms and I did not awaken till the sun came through the wide windows of my bedroom.

CHAPTER FIFTEEN

April found me the next morning outside with the satellite and office people, instructing them as to how I wanted everything arranged. Wiring the huge old house was going to be quite a job and I had completely forgotten to mention the plans to April after the incident yesterday.

She had showered, eaten, and had come looking for me outside where the men were trying to find the best locations to place the equipment without changing the façade of the ancient house.

She was wearing her usual American jeans, white shirt, and white Keds, with her long hair loosely braided to one side. She had a mug of coffee with her and handed it to me.

"Not my 'weak-ass' coffee. Mrs. Gregory made this for you. By the way I think we can mark her off our list of potential leaks. She thinks the sun and moon set by you. I spent some time in the kitchen with her talking about your family and her family. No, has to be someone else."

I took a deep drink of the thick and rich black coffee. I nodded my head. I had never considered Mrs. Gregory as Alex's confidante. I remembered how rude he had to been to her as an adolescent. No, April was right. Mrs. Gregory was on our side.

"I'm having internet, television, and a satellite phone system installed. I can't work when we're here with just a land line. Your brother might be very unhappy being left alone to make decisions and I miss working."

She smiled and laced her arm through mine.

"Good. Will I be able to Skype my folks and friends as well?"

I laughed and nodded.

"To your heart's content."

We heard the front door open and close and glanced over to see Alex heading our way. I took a deep breath and wished he would just go back to Edinburgh. No such luck.

"Well, Gordon, finally bringing the house into the 21st century. About damn time."

He turned to April and I realized that Charlotte's Cheshire cat smile was on his face. I suddenly wanted to punch him, but April must have sensed my growing tension and squeezed my arm.

"Ms. Norris, would you like to go into the village and have lunch at the pub as you promised? Especially since Gordon here is going to be extremely busy today."

I really wanted to hit him, but April's hand was squeezing my arm even more tightly.

"Certainly, Alex. I'll join you in the great hall in five minutes."

"My dear lady, you are truly kind," he said, his face arranged in a smirk as he left us.

April stood on her tiptoes and kissed my cheek.

"Reconnaissance mission. Nothing else. I want to find out his plans and who's feeding him information. You must trust me. Don't let the delusions tell you otherwise. I love only you," she said.

I wrapped my one free arm around her and drew her to me, kissing her deeply and long enough for the work crew to pause and stare at us.

"I think we're being a little too demonstrative for the crew," she said and giggled.

"Ah, to hell with it. I'm sick of not being able to show you just how much I do love you. Now, go spy on my cousin and bring back a good report," I said, slapping her backside as she moved away from me.

She gave a little shimmy in my direction and shook her finger at me, smiling.

Sheila was right. April was the best thing that had ever happened to me. But schizophrenia was the worst. Even a normal man would worry when his love was being subtly wooed by a man who was his enemy. A schizophrenic could see even darker intentions there.

"Well, of course, you should be worried. Wow, look at that tight little ass. I bet Alex will be touching that at some point today. He's had a lot more practice than you at seduction, after all."

I found Will standing next to me in the same tennis sweater, although there were streaks of blood on it. I stared at the sweater in horror, remembering Charlotte's body lying in the window.

"Oh, she's still with us. You can't kill us off so easily, but try not to be so bloody violent next time. Really, you could go upstairs and have some great sex with old Charl while Alex seduces that tight little thing. In fact, I may jump in his body and do it for him."

I stared horrified at what I had just heard. 'Jump' into his body? Could he really hurt April that way? Could he attack her?

I didn't say a word, but I'm sure the expression on my face gave away my thoughts as Will merrily headed off in the direction of the great hall.

Delusions. Hallucinations. I chanted the words over and over in my head and tried to calm myself. I walked over to where the men were working and began to immerse myself in their progress in order to forget the words I had just heard.

After lunch, I went upstairs to shower and change and went to the front parlor to join my other cousins and their respective spouses. They were having tea, thankfully not orange pekoe. We sat and discussed the changes to the house and I told them that whenever they wished to have a weekend in the country to make use of the place.

"When April and I go back to the States, I'd be happy to know that Burnock was not sitting here empty of the laughter of our family."

Sheila smiled at that and said that she would love to bring her girls up to go riding and see where their family roots were. Samuel agreed with her, although he said that he thought that it might be awhile before he and Tamara could make it up.

"New babies and many changes," he laughed.

"When is April due back here? I thought they were only having lunch," Tamara inquired.

I tried to make light of their lateness, but I was beginning to worry myself. It was nearing dinner and dusk would soon be falling. I thought of Will's words about 'jumping' into Alex and shivered.

Mrs. MacCurdy entered the parlor and asked when we expected everyone for dinner.

"Mrs. Gregory is insistent on knowing when to have dinner served."

I almost snorted at her remark. I sincerely doubted that Mrs. Gregory was being 'insistent' and I thought that Mrs. MacCurdy might be the inquisitive one. She had always been attached to Alex and had doted on him as a child. For some reason, she had not showered the same affection on my other cousins and myself.

"Mrs. MacCurdy, please inform Mrs. Gregory that

our usual dinner hour will be perfectly fine. Oh, and there's no need for you to stay. You may retire for the evening, just be mindful of the new wiring being placed in the house. I'm having indoor security cameras added as well as exterior."

"Wouldn't want you to slip," I said and smiled.

"Very good, sir," she replied and almost harrumphed as she left the room.

"What the hell is bothering her?" Samuel asked. "She seems more irritable than usual."

I shrugged my shoulders and looked to the windows to see if I could see Alex's car nearing the house. I was surprised to see the headlights speeding erratically toward the front drive. I jumped up and headed to the front door to meet them.

As I exited the house, I was shocked to see April open the driver's door and extricate herself from the car. Her entire body was as taut as a violin bow.

"We need to talk. As soon as we possibly can without arousing suspicion," she whispered to me.

"Someone might want to assist Alex to his room. He's very drunk and I had quite a time trying to drive his idiotically complex sports car back here," she said to everyone else.

Samuel and Andrew volunteered to help Alex and the rest of us went into the house and back into the parlor.

Sheila poured a small glass of brandy and handed it to April, looking at me as she did so. I shrugged my shoulders and sat next to April as she began to relax.

"We went straight to the pub and never left. I drank tonic water, but Alex went through an entire bottle of Scotch. I felt he was too drunk so I had some of the men at the pub help me get him into that ridiculous Jag and I very slowly drove home. I was scared to death of driving on the wrong side of the road. I drove so slowly that people were actually blasting their horns at me."

She looked at me and smiled.

"You must give me some driving lessons here. I'm not used to narrow roads or cars that are the opposite of our American ones."

I hugged her and laughed as Samuel and Andrew reentered the parlor.

"Well, he's down for the night. Kept mumbling about someone named 'Will'," Samuel said.

I whirled around at the mention of Will's name and

April sat up and whispered, "That's what I need to tell you."

I inhaled and stood and smiled.

"Let's go ahead and have dinner. We don't want Mrs. Gregory's delicious meal to go to waste."

I noticed as we ate that April's hands were still shaking. I took one of them in mine and clasped it gently so that she would know that I was there for her.

That night none of us stayed up and we all went upstairs after carrying the dinner dishes into the kitchen where one of the new maids was waiting. She insisted on finishing the cleaning up and I gladly handed it over to her. I realized that I hadn't seen her before and had it not been for April, I would have stopped to inquire more about her.

By the time we went into my bedroom, April was almost in tears. I noticed that Mrs. MacCurdy had April's bed ready and mine as well, as if to tell us to stay in our own rooms. I was getting a bit angry with her and I decided that I would talk to father about her presumptive attitude the next day. She was surly and often rude and I distrusted her extremely passive-aggressive behavior.

I led April to my bath and helped her to undress so

she could soak in the oversized bathtub and talk to me about the afternoon's events.

By the time I had returned with linens and her bathrobe, she was deep in the tub with bubbles floating almost to her collarbones.

"Gordon, you may think you're ill, but Alex is crazy with resentment and anger. You really need to get him away from here as soon as possible. At first, he seemed his usual smarmy self, but somewhere after the first drink, he became belligerent with the others in the pub and, well, a little too hands on with me."

I raised my eyebrows and had her lean forward so I could scrub her back.

"Oh, that feels wonderful. Sorry, where was I? Oh, he kept trying to put his hands on my legs and breasts and I actually slapped him at one point. That was when one of the men we met the other day came over and told him to 'Keep his hands to his self'."

"He told the man to piss off, but his hands stopped their roaming. Anyway, that was when he began to rant about you hiding some sort of illness, that you'd never have an heir, and that he was going to make sure you never inherited your title or money."

She turned to me and put her hands on mine.

"Gordon, I've never in my life been afraid of a man. I grew up with brothers and you know I know how to defend myself, but he's, there's something dangerously *wrong* about him."

She laid back in the tub and looked up at the ceiling.

"I'm afraid of him. I don't ever want to be alone with him again."

She sat up and the bubbles that surrounded her began to float away. Even in the brightly white tiled bathroom, her skin glowed. Had I not been so concerned by her words, I would have stripped and joined her. I had a momentary vision of making love to her there and shook my head.

"Please, Gordon, I'm really afraid he's going to do something more than just come at you over your illness. I'm afraid he's going to do something bad to you. His talk of your never having an heir or taking your inheritance. It was so wrong."

I held up her robe and helped her out of the oversized tub, trying to ease her fears.

"I thought I was the one who was paranoid," I laughed as helped her to dry off.

"He just wasn't like the man from the last few days and the more he drank, the worse he became."

She went into my bedroom, dropped the bathrobe in the floor and climbed into my bed. I stood there for a minute trying to decide what to do. I wanted to undress and join her, but instead I picked up her robe, hung it up in my bathroom to dry, and continued to listen as she spoke.

"It was when he started telling me to call him 'Will' that I really became afraid. How could he know about 'Will'? You've told no one but Sheila and me. But it got worse when he was almost done with the bottle and he told me you were here 'having at it' with 'good old Charl'. That was when I got the men at the pub to help me get him in the car and I started back here. He mumbled about you some more in the car before he passed out, but I couldn't understand what he was saying. Gaelic incomprehensibility on my part, I suppose."

I sat down on the bed next to her and was even more afraid than she could imagine by what she had just told me. It was as if Will had really 'jumped' into Alex's body and taken over. How was that even possible? Will was my delusion and my delusions couldn't take over another person, especially when that person was around other people and not me. It made absolutely no sense.

"April, I haven't a clue about any of this. You and Sheila are the only ones who know Will's name, though there are others in the family who obviously know Charlotte's name. But why would Alex take on Will's persona and threaten me in front of an entire pub full of people? I just don't understand."

She wrapped her arms around me and turned me towards her and began to unbutton my shirt.

"I don't want to think about Alex or Will or anyone else but you right now. Come to bed with me. I'm cold without you next to me."

I climbed into the bed with her and struggled out of my clothes. I began to make love to her, kissing her throat, her breasts and shoulders as she moved her hands to below my waist, stroking me and leading me towards her when she stopped.

"Wait, do you want a condom?" she asked.

"No, love, I want nothing but you," I said and softly pushed my way into her.

We made love more than once that night and I prayed for the first time that we might conceive a child together. I wanted to marry her and fill Burnock with our children. For one of the few times in my life, I did not feel ill. I felt alive and unafraid of a future with her.

CHAPTER SIXTEEN

We awoke together in my bed, our bodies still tangled together. The early sunrise had lit the cream walls of the room in beautiful pastel shades of yellow and pink. I watched her sleep, her eyelids moving rapidly and I realized that she was dreaming.

I decided to bring her from her own 'Dreamville' and awaken her in my bed by gently raining kisses down upon her, touching her in ways that I knew would arouse her.

Her eyes fluttered open and she suddenly sat up in bed, holding the sheet to her chest and sidling away from me.

"April, love, it's alright. You were just dreaming."

She took a few seconds before her eyes focused on my face.

"I had the most horrible dream. A woman had tied me up and was holding me at gun point when you walked in, but it wasn't you. You began to touch me and it felt awful."

I sat upright next to her in the bed.

"Was it in your parent's home?" I asked, afraid of her response, but she shook her head.

"No. Yes. No. I don't know where it was."

She stopped and reached out and touched my chest.

"A nightmare. I'm sorry," she said as she hugged me tightly.

I could feel her heart beating fast against my own chest and I stroked her hair, trying to soothe her the way she had soothed me so many times when I had come in and out of my 'Dreamville'. I felt a dampness on my chest and held her away from me to see that she was crying.

"Oh, my love, don't. No one's going to hurt you. This is all from that mess with Alex yesterday. I'm going to make sure he leaves today. Enough is enough. I also need to contact my father and let him know what's been going on here. I'm his only heir and he should be made aware of what Alex said in the pub. I'm sure everyone in the village is talking about it now."

I jumped from the bed and went to shower and shave before beginning my lengthy lists of changes I had planned for myself and my home. When I returned from the bathroom to dress, I saw that April had not moved from the bed and was staring out the window at the fields around the house.

"Gordon, where are we going to live? Here? New York?"

I was buttoning a blue work shirt as I watched the worry on her face.

"Where do you want to live? This will all be mine one day, but wherever you are is my home."

I sat down on the bed next to her and bounced a bit in an attempt to lighten her mood.

"Antarctica? Miami? Italy? I know – Beijing!"

She laughed and kissed me.

"Seriously, Gordon. I love it here, but I've never been frightened anywhere, well, except for the third floor of my parents' home, but something here 'feels' wrong right now. I just can't pinpoint what it is. *And* our parents are in New York and Connecticut."

"Oh, ignore me. I'm still a little jumpy from yesterday and from that dream," she continued.

"Let me take care of everything today. I'll call father later today and go over everything with him. We'll have a plan of action then."

I kissed her again, went to the door, and walked out it and right into my own hellish version of 'Dreamville' – Charlotte's Kensington home or my former home. At this point I had no idea what to think.

"Bloody hell!" I yelled and turned back to try to return to April, but the door to my bedroom in Burnock had vanished and was replaced by the foyer of the Kensington house. And of course, there she was, coming down the staircase towards me.

"Lover, whatever is the problem? It's too early in the morning to be stomping around and cursing. God, my head hurts. I absolutely hate being jet-lagged."

She was wearing a man's paisley silk robe that I realized had been mine or I had thought was mine. It was barely closed and her blonde hair lightly brushed her collar bones above those incredible breasts.

Well, at least I gave her a good body when I dreamt her up. But I became irritated that I was aroused by that body. I wanted to be back with April, not here in my Dreamville version of London.

"What in the world are you wearing?" she commented as she sat down at her dining table where someone had laid out two place settings, toast, jam, and, oh God, orange Pekoe tea. She picked up The Times and glanced at the headlines without looking back at me.

"Truly, Gordon, are you going to work as a landscaper today? Oh, my God. Another delusion. Well, at least you're not dressed as a Beefeater."

She took a bite of toast and sipped at the tea before she realized that I had not moved from the foyer.

"For heaven's sake, will you sit down and eat? Stop being a ridiculous fool. You are not a day laborer or whatever you're dressed to do."

I still did not move, but I did close my eyes and thought of delusions and hallucinations and April. I had to get back to April.

Charlotte walked over the where I was standing and grabbed my hand and put it on her right breast.

"I am no delusion! Stop it now! I am real, not this Pamela April person you're always pining for. Feel my breast! This is real!"

I opened my eyes and stared into her dark blue eyes. She had just said a version of what April had said to me in New York. I was suddenly afraid that this might be real and April was my 'Dreamville'. My stomach churned at the thought that my illness might be so advanced that I no longer could tell the difference between reality and insanity.

I glanced down and saw my hand still holding her right breast and quickly withdrew it from her robe. I could feel my face burning in embarrassment. I felt as if I had just betrayed April by touching Charlotte's breast.

"Enough," Charlotte said and took my hand and using surprising strength, pulled me up the staircase behind her.

"Wait, Charlotte, this . . . I can't"

She dragged me into a bedroom I recognized as one from when I had thought I had been engaged to a real woman. Everything was so real. My head began to pound as I found her ripping at my shirt and unbuttoning my Levis.

I pushed her back and held her at arms' length. I pushed her onto the bed and her robe fell open to reveal her very generous endowments. She smiled that Cheshire cat smile and I remembered Alex smiling that way. I pulled my clothing back together, ran down the steps and swung open the front door to find myself in the upper hall of Burnock House.

I fell forward against the bedroom door and almost cried in relief. The door in front of me suddenly opened and for a brief moment I feared that Charlotte would be there, but it was my sweet April, wrapped in a bed sheet, helping me into my room to sit.

CHAPTER SEVENTEEN

I sat on the bedside with her next to me and rubbed my pounding head. Without my noticing it, she had gone for a glass of water and my medication. I took it from her without a word and quickly swallowed the pills.

"Gordon, you have to take the medication. You can't forget. I need you to be strong, to fight this."

I nodded my head and buried my face in her black curls. I was so glad to see her. For a moment in the bedroom with Charlotte in Dreamville, I had doubted her existence. I sighed and told her what had happened, even Charlotte's similar statements about April being the hallucination and that Charlotte was the real woman. I did not tell April about Charlotte's attempt to seduce me or my own unprompted desire to return her advances.

April sat next to me and bit her lip, studying the

door, deep in thought about what I had told her.

"I think there's a simple answer as to who is real and who is not. Who did you know first? Who does your family know? Gordon, it's me. I knew your family before you knew me. You knew my brother before you knew me."

She turned to me on the bed and sat cross-legged, holding my arm.

"It's simple logic. Think about it. You didn't take your meds this morning and you were angry over Alex's behavior and upset after I told you my nightmare. And you had to confront him – something you were loath to do."

"Tell me, when this Charlotte was telling you she was real, did she place your hand on her breasts?"

I rolled my eyes and laid back upon the bed, not wanting to see her face as I told her yes.

"Exactly!" she exclaimed.

"And how did I say the truth to you about my existence? Think about it. We had made love and I was standing nude before you. I placed your hands on my breasts and told you that I was real, not an illusion."

I threw my arm across my eyes and I could feel the

meds beginning to ease the pounding in my head. April lay down next to me and curled up along side my body.

"We have to do some things to keep you on an even keel, especially making sure you take your meds regularly for now, no matter how much you hate them. We can't risk Alex gaining control of Burnock."

"Secondly, I don't believe for a second that 'Will' possessed him. More likely someone has been . . ." her voice faltered and faded to silence. I looked at her as she raised a finger to her lips.

"I'm going to bathe. Why don't you rest while I do," she said loudly while instead of undressing to bathe, she began to dress.

I watched her in puzzlement as she pointed around the room and mimicked holding something to her ear, as if to tell me that someone could be listening. I sat up in bed, surprised at her assumption and looked around the room. Could Alex have had the room bugged? Was that how he was getting his information?

I thought of someone listening to our conversation and realized that they had also probably been eavesdropping on us during our lovemaking. It made me sick and it made me furious. I could feel the heat on my face rising from my anger.

April held her finger up again and led me towards the door and out of the room.

"We can't take a chance on talking in either bedroom," she said.

"I want to strangle him," I replied.

"No, Gordon, that'll only make it worse. You can't accuse him without proof. And God help me, and don't get angry, but he might not be the one who's doing it."

I stepped back from her.

"April, the others wouldn't, couldn't . . ."

She moved to me and spoke softly.

"Think about it, Gordon. Who is next in line if both you and Alex are out of the picture? Good God, I'm afraid to trust anyone but you right now."

I shook my head. "No, it can't be Sheila or Samuel. I can't believe it. They've always known that I would do anything for them."

"That's just it, Gordon. Maybe they don't want to be beholden to you. Have you checked into their financial situations? Alex has his own money and will inherit from his mother. Mrs. Gregory told me that. Are the others in stable shape?"

I stared down the hall towards the east wing where they were probably rising for the day. Could it be possible that they were pitting Alex and myself against one another? I just could not believe it.

I took a deep breath and then looked at the doors into our rooms.

"Well, I'll find out today if anyone is spying on us. I'll pull the foreman off the work today and have him sweep the room. In fact, stay here until he comes back so that no one has a chance to go in the rooms."

She nodded and looked down at the floor. As I was about to head down the staircase, I heard her say "I'm sorry, Gordon."

Twenty minutes later the foreman was in our rooms and we were entering the dining hall to have breakfast. Everyone else slowly trickled in, with Alex bringing up the rear. He looked as if he had a first class hangover and I couldn't resist the chance to taunt him.

"Good morning, all!" I said loudly.

Alex winced and walked as far away from me as he could. He started to sit where he usually sat next to April and was surprised to find her next to me with the place setting next to her removed. He went to the far end of the table and pushed away his food from in front of him, drinking only water.

"Alex, you'll find your car safe and sound in the garage. April drove you home without any damage to it."

He winced again and nodded a thanks in our general direction. The rest of the family looked on at the little mini-drama being performed. I noticed that April was watching their faces closely, looking for any clues that someone other than Alex might be plotting against me. I squeezed her hand and smiled as I began to eat a larger than normal breakfast.

April's logic had relieved some of my stress, as well as the meds I had taken.

Everyone at the table but myself jumped when the sounds of a drill began winding its way into the room.

"Good grief, Gordon, must they do that at such an ungodly hour?" Alex asked.

"So sorry, Alex, but I wanted everything done this week. I need to be in touch with the New York office as soon as possible. Weren't you saying yesterday that you were glad I was bringing the house into the 21st century?"

He threw his napkin on the table and headed back towards the door to the kitchen. When he passed through the door, he missed the giggles emanating from the others at the table, although the pounding that began next made Tamara jump.

"Sorry, Tamara. You know, you and the family may want to head back to Edinburgh today. It's going to be rather noisy and dusty here for the rest of the week."

I was not prepared for the objection from Sheila.

"Nonsense, Gordon. A little noise won't bother us."

I glanced at April who appeared to be studying her oatmeal as if it were an ancient relic.

"Sheila, I think it's really for the best. April will be working with me during the renovation and neither of us will be available."

"But Gordon, I thought we had discussed . . ."

I cut her short. I had to get them all out of the house.

"I know, Sheila dear, but we have so much work to do. It would really be terribly unfair. I'll have Mr. Ferguson bring your cars round after breakfast so you can get an early start. I'm sure you can be packed by then," I said closing the subject.

I felt rather bad as I noticed that Sheila's eyes were welling with tears. She had been so good in keeping my secrets this past week. But, I knew that this was the only way to secure the truth.

"Please, perhaps in a few weeks you can bring the girls up and we can have a weekend together," I said, trying to ease the blow of literally tossing them out.

Just as I spoke, the foreman came to the door and asked to speak with me. I excused myself and was surprised to find April following me.

"Mr. Stewart, I found this in the flowers on the bed table," he said handing me a small device the looked as if it were some sort of camera and microphone.

"I disabled it, but I would think that more than one is here in the house. Would you like me to check the rest of the house?"

I nodded as I stared at the tiny device and then stopped him as he walked away.

"Do the guest rooms and the staff rooms first. I want to know who's been on the other end of this thing. And do it as quickly as you can. I'll try to delay things to give you some time."

I shook my head and headed back into the dining hall. April's face was pale with shock. I don't think she really thought her little conspiracy theory had been anything more than just a theory. She was having trouble coming to terms with the situation. Surprisingly, I was not. Perhaps my illness had prepared me for it. I didn't know.

"You know, there's no reason for everyone to rush off this morning. Why don't we drive to the village this morning before everyone's off?" I smiled broadly as I spoke, trying to convince them of my sincerity of wanting their company.

"Gordon, if you don't mind, I think I'm going to beg off. The morning sickness is bad this morning," Tamara said.

April went to her side and placed her hand on Tamara's shoulder.

"I'll stay with her. Maybe we can rest in the parlor with some toast and tea," she said.

"Excellent. I'll have Ferguson bring a car around and I'll grab Alex. A nice trip before everyone departs."

The others looked a bit nonplussed, but Sheila seemed calmer now than she had earlier. I only hoped that the foreman could find the receiver before everyone left. I thought of someone watching April and me in our intimate moments and I struggled to maintain my smile.

As we filed out into the great hall and Alex straggled in from the kitchen, everyone went outside and clambered into one of the large estate vans.

I kissed April and whispered, "Be strong and don't let her out of your sight."

She nodded and walked over to Tamara and linked her arm in Tamara's. I don't know who was more frightened then – she or I.

CHAPTER EIGHTEEN

It was nearing lunch when we arrived back at Burnock. I saw that April was sitting in the garden, alone, and I wondered what had transpired during our trip to the village.

While the others went inside to pack, I walked into the garden and sat down next to April.

"Well?"

She held her hand out and there were six more tiny cameras there. She clasped her hand into a fist and used it to wipe the tears from her eyes.

"I don't know whether to be angry or sick, Gordon. They were everywhere. And someone watched us . . . watched us together. But the worst is that the foreman didn't find a receiver. Whoever planted these could have recorded us making love."

I grabbed the cameras from her hand and walked fast into the house, finding everyone still in the great hall, talking. April ran after me. I slammed the front doors and everyone there hushed.

"April, get the staff in here. Now. All of them." I said, my voice stiff with anger. "I'd like everyone else to have a seat in the parlor."

Alex stepped forward angrily.

"Gordon, I've about had it with your manners and attitude. May I remind you again that you're not the laird yet?"

"Alex, get in the fucking parlor before I throw you in there."

He stepped away and everyone moved as a group toward the parlor when I realized that Tamara was not with them.

"Where's Tamara?"

I heard April coming up behind me.

"She's on her way. She was lying down upstairs."

As everyone, including the staff, made their way into the parlor, April stood behind me as if she wanted to disappear. She was so humiliated by what had been found and what had not been found.

"I want to know where the receiver is to these and who is responsible for them," I said, throwing the tiny cameras on the table in front of them.

"What are those?" Tamara said.

"They're cameras," April said, stepping forward, wiping the remaining tears from her cheeks. "Cameras that were used to spy on Gordon and myself. God, they were even used to film us in our bedrooms!"

Everyone in the room seemed to be in shock.

"Who would do this?" Tamara asked. "It's . . . it's indecent."

"Yes, it is. But what's worse is that we did not find the receiver. Now who the fuck did this? I guarantee you that I will find out. These things can be traced. Someone had better own up to this or I'll have them arrested."

I turned to April.

"April, call the village police inspector and ask him if he could come over to the house."

I then turned backed to the room full of people as April went to the telephone in the great hall to make her call.

"Last chance."

"For God's sake, Gordon, you can't think that I, that

we did this. It's sick," Sheila said.

"Yes, it's quite sick, but someone in this house did it. And they will pay dearly for it. I can keep this in the family now if I get the receiver and any recordings that were made, but if I don't, I'll find out the truth and God help the person who did this then."

"Maybe 'Will' or Charlotte did it," Alex said.

"You bastard. I knew it was you," I said as I charged at him. Sheila and Andrew grabbed my arms to hold me back.

He leaned back in the leather club chair and lit a cigarette and laughed.

"I wish I had thought of it. I'd love to see the lovely April having at it."

Samuel joined Andrew and Sheila and he pushed me into a seat.

"Perhaps you did it. You're the schizoid, here, not us," Alex continued and blew smoke at Tamara. She waved it away and moved to Samuel's side.

"Oh, please, we all know he's mentally unstable. Even the staff knows about it, don't they, Mrs. MacCurdy?"

April had returned to the parlor and said that the

village inspector was on his way to the house.

"April, my dear, Gordon probably filmed it so he could relive all those moments with you when you leave him. After all, you wouldn't be the first woman to dump him."

April looked at me. "What's he saying, Gordon?"

"Nonsense. He planted the damn things and is trying to make it seem as though I did it because of my illness."

"Illness? Is that what you call it? How about stark raving bonkers? Mad as a hatter? Or perhaps a more clinical description – a paranoid schizophrenic?" Alex replied.

April took my hand and held it tightly, as if to shield us from his accusations.

"Oh please, will someone else acknowledge what we all know?" Alex said, glancing around the room.

"Gordon, could you. . . you wouldn't, would you?" Samuel asked.

"For heaven's sake, Samuel, don't be a fool," Sheila said. "What would make you think that Gordon would do something so stupid and then accuse someone else?"

Samuel blushed as if either ashamed of his actions or embarrassed by his words.

April looked at me and we both knew then that she might have been right about the person not being Alex.

I leaned forward and said sadly, "Oh Samuel, how could you?"

CHAPTER NINETEEN

"How could I what?" Samuel asked. "I would never do something so vile."

"Oh, Gordon, stop trying to play innocent," Alex said.

Mrs. MacCurdy stepped forward and stood in front of Alex.

"Mr. Alex, shame on you! Mr. Stewart couldna hae placed those things. He dinna hae taime," she paused and tried to regain her composure, allowing the Scottish burr to fade.

"He arrived two days after the rest of the family. He and Ms. April had not even planned to come. But you and the family had planned to be here."

I stared at Mrs. MacCurdy and then at April.

"What are you saying, Mrs. MacCurdy?"

"I'm sorry, sir. I should have said something when you arrived, but you seemed so upset. They," she said spreading her arm to indicate the rest of the family, "They had planned their visit weeks before your father contacted us."

I did not know what to say. Could they all have conspired against me or was it my own sickness? I could not accept that my family would do this to me.

April continued to stand beside me, defiant as Mrs. MacCurdy announced her revelation. She glared at my family in disgust and hatred, but she looked to Sheila first.

"How could you? We trusted you."

Sheila shook her head and sat on the sofa, her eyes wet with tears.

"April, I would never have done this. You and Gordon must believe me. Never. And what reason would I have had? Andrew and I have nothing to gain. Please."

April took a deep breath and looked at the remaining staff – the new housemaid, Mrs. Gregory, Ferguson, and the grounds manager.

"Someone here did it. Maybe more than one. I suspect that it would have been easier had someone had a partner."

"Bloody hell, she's as crazy as he is!" Alex exclaimed.

Mrs. MacCurdy slapped him and he jumped to his feet.

"If you ever touch me again you old bitch, you'll spend the rest of your days serving other prisoners."

"Would everyone just sit down," I said. "We'll just let the inspector sort this out when he arrives. Frankly, I'm tired of the whole thing."

Everyone took seats around the large room, no one looking at anyone else. Only April continued to stand next to me. I lifted her hand and asked her to sit as well, but she shook her head. I had seen that defiance so many times, from the chair Nazi incident to her refusal to leave my side at JFK. The rest of the people in that room had no idea just how strong she was. Some of them probably thought her kindness was weakness. They could not have been more wrong.

At one point Alex walked over to the garden windows and opened them and lit another cigarette, this time seeming to be considerate of Tamara's pregnancy. Andrew poured a brandy for Sheila, whose hands trembled ever so slightly. Samuel sat slumped on a sofa next to Tamara. No one spoke a word, especially the staff.

I looked over to the new housemaid and was about to ask Mrs. MacCurdy the girl's name when a sharp knock was heard at the front doors. I excused myself and went into the great hall, closing the parlor doors behind me. I opened the front doors to find Will standing before me with Charlotte next to him.

I stumbled back and found myself standing in Charlotte's Kensington house. I closed my eyes and tripped, falling backward to the floor of the London house's foyer.

Charlotte's blonde hair was streaked with strands of dried brown blood. The streaks matched the blood on the tennis sweater that Will wore.

I closed my eyes again, hoping that when I opened them that I would be back at Burnock, but instead I found myself sitting on a very ugly green sofa in my half-furnished New York apartment.

I jumped up and looked for my mobile. It was on the kitchen counter. Just as I picked it up it began to vibrate. I saw April's name appear on the screen and quickly pushed the 'accept' button.

"April, are you alright?"

For a moment there was silence on the other end of the phone, then I heard her voice.

"Yes, Mr. Stewart. I'm fine, but someone was just in my apartment. I couldn't reach Rick and I thought he might be with you."

"I'll be there right away. Stay in the lobby with Frank."

"How did you know . . ." she began to ask but her voice trailed off.

"I'm on my way." I turned the mobile off and ran to the elevator. I knew exactly where in Dreamville I was. I had been through this particular episode before, but I wondered how I had gotten from London to New York by closing my eyes.

Just as I heard the elevator nearing my floor, I suddenly felt the presence of someone else behind me. I whirled around and saw Charlotte standing there in that red bloody dress.

"You can't save her and you can't help yourself. Face it, lover, you're stuck with us. We're never going to leave either of you alone and you know how this will end. You've already been there before."

I ran to her and grabbed her by the throat and began

to squeeze as I screamed out, "No! No! No!"

I could feel the warmth of her skin, smell the perfume rising from her breasts, even feel the bones beneath my hands as they encircled her throat.

She just laughed and tossed her head back.

"Squeeze away, lover. When are you going to realize that you can't rid yourself of me?" she asked and I suddenly found my hands grasping the air in front of me, her form vanished completely.

Behind me, the elevator doors opened and I stumbled into the car, shaken by what had just happened. As the elevator descended to the lobby, all I could do was wonder if I were mad beyond salvation. Everything seemed to be heading back towards that horrible dream that had led me home to Burnock again. The dream where I had brutally raped and murdered the woman I loved.

CHAPTER TWENTY

Just as with this particular previous visit to Dreamville, I found April trembling in fear in the lobby of her apartment building. I wanted to comfort her as familiarly as I would the April in my real life, the April who knew everything about me, the April who had shared my life and love; but, I knew that was not possible. In fact, I wondered if I told her everything if she would run from me. A sensible woman would.

So the routine of Dreamville ran its course, with the police officers, the video of the woman. Everything the same except that this time I realized the woman in the video was Charlotte. Although her face could not be seen, her movements, her walk were those of the woman I now knew as a delusion from my illness.

I was still puzzled by how these things could be

happening. I recognized Charlotte and Will as products of my sickness. I even seemed to accept the quick shifts of time and location that only occurred within my mind. But what I feared, what confused me, were the increasing violence and belligerence in the hallucinations, including the "jumping", as Will had phrased it, into people and events where I was not present.

I believe what frightened me the most was what Charlotte had said in the apartment – that I knew what was going to happen and that there was nothing I could do to prevent it and that she and Will would be with me forever.

While I was 32 in this version of Dreamville, I knew that in reality that I was approaching my 26th birthday. Could I bear a lifetime with the monsters I had created? Could I bear a lifetime without April? And most importantly, how could I ever live in a world where I had murdered my love?

I waited for this time in Dreamville to play itself out like a bad episode of a television series, knowing that the end of this particular series arc was almost over. I observed the detectives and wondered if they were real people or delusionary characters in my little psychological dramas. I knew that Frank was a real person. He was the doorman at our apartment on Central Park. Why had I chosen to transpose him here?

As the detectives continued to repeat their same lines, to behave as they had before, I walked over to the doors of the building and looked out onto the streets of Soho. A grey sleet was falling, icing the sidewalks and streets, the strong winds pushing through the Manhattan canyons making people move quickly. I peered into the distance and saw the red dress Charlotte was wearing, with Will standing next to her as if they, too, were waiting for realities to shift.

I turned back to April and she looked up at me. At that moment I saw something else that I had never seen before – she was aware that something was hideously out of sync with our lives. For the first time, I saw in April's eyes the knowledge that this not real, that we were both trapped in some sort of cycle from which neither of us could escape.

I went to her immediately and led her away from the detectives and Frank and to the elevator to her apartment. She clung tightly to my arm and neither of us listened nor answered the complaints from the three people we left standing in the lobby. I wrapped her in my arms and could feel her body shivering beneath the silk robe she wore.

She looked up into my eyes and I bent my head and kissed her, tenderly at first and then harder and deeper as our need for each other grew. When I saw we had reached her floor and the elevator doors opened, I swept her up in my arms and carried her down the haunted hall. She never spoke and I never put her down until we had reached her antique bed.

Tonight I was going to change Dreamville. I would change the cycle. I would make love to her for the first time and for the hundredth. I saw in her eyes that I was no more a stranger to her as a lover than she was to me.

Charlotte would not burst in as she had in the shop. Will would not appear. Nothing would stop us as we loved one another. I would not allow it. Even when my mobile and then hers began ringing, I only stopped long enough to disable them, throw them from the bedroom and go back to her.

She had removed the robe and had laid back on the yellow silk as her black hair flowed around her. I stripped and began to kiss and stroke her body, feeling and knowing the contours of her breasts, her inner thighs, the gentle curve of her neck as I had known it for so long.

And she responded as if she had made love to me so many times before now. She pulled me upon her and whispered my name as she kissed my chest and my arms.

"Gordon, make it all stop. Love me and save us."

Her eyes locked with mine as she spoke and I knew then, for the first time in my life, that I was not mad, that I was not schizophrenic and that whatever was happening to me was happening to her as well. Wherever I traveled, I took her with me or she took me. Whatever Dreamville was, it was not an illness. It was real.

CHAPTER TWENTY-ONE

I came out of Dreamville and found myself on the floor next to the front doors of Burnock. April was kneeling next to me just as Sheila and Andrew entered the great hall.

"He slipped on the rug and hit his head. Sheila, could you have Mrs. MacCurdy get something cold to put on his head and Andrew would you mind getting the door?" she asked them sweetly, as she held my head in her lap.

Both of them quickly went to their respective tasks and as they did, she whispered to me.

"Don't say anything about what just happened. They won't believe us."

"You remember? New York? Charlotte?"

"Everything," she hissed and helped me to sit up.

By that time Andrew and the inspector from the village had reached us. I realized the inspector was a boy I had been good friends with as a child. Now a man. Sean Craig. Sean rushed to where April and I were in the floor.

"Well, Gordon, not exactly the reunion I expected," he said. "Are you alright?"

I grimaced a bit as I touched the back of my head, but nodded to let him know I was okay.

"You must be the incumbent Mrs. Stewart," he laughed and held out his hand to April. "I'm Sean Craig, a very old friend of this rather clumsy man."

"Pleased to meet you, Sean. Could you help us into the parlor? I think Gordon hit his head fairly hard when the rug slid and he fell."

Sean and Andrew helped me to my feet and as we were walking to the front parlor, he stopped and looked back at the rug.

"Didn't your mother always keep those non-slip things under all the small carpets? I seem to remember her ordering them for the whole house after we both crashed into one of her tables as children."

He was right. Mother had placed them under any carpet smaller than a room size Persian. Sean and I had been running through the hall just as her guests had arrived for tea one afternoon and we had slid on a smaller carpet and had literally upset her tea cart and made a great mess of her event.

I looked towards one of the other carpets and could barely see the rubber padding beneath it.

"You're right, Sean. That's odd. I could have sworn that pad was there before today."

"The others seem to still be intact," he said, pointing to the carpet I had looked at.

"You're lucky you don't have a cracked skull," he said as we went into the room.

April helped me back to my chair while Sean introduced himself to those in the room who did not know him. She held my hand so tightly that at one point I had to take my other hand and ease it slightly away. She blushed and went back to her position beside my chair.

Sean picked up one of the devices and examined it.

"So, this is part of the problem," he said. "Hmm. There seems to be a serial number on it so it shouldn't be hard to trace."

"And you found these in your personal rooms and the study?"

I nodded. "But no receiver or computer, at least that we've been able to find either here or on the grounds. They could be satellite linked, but I don't think so as we just began the installation yesterday."

Sean examined the other devices and then put them into a small clear plastic bag that he put in his jacket pocket.

"So, who wants to talk first? I think that this may be the only chance Gordon is going to give anyone to walk away."

I looked around the room and no one would look at Sean or April or me. Suddenly Mrs. MacCurdy stood and faced Sean.

"I'll talk to ye first. I've no taime to waste on such stupidity. I'll tell ye everything I know." She made no attempt at tempering her burr this time.

"Gordon, may I use your study?"

I nodded and pointed the way.

"Don't worry. I remember getting in trouble with your father over a game of hide and seek in there," he laughed. "Oh, and as to the rest of you. Don't be trying to leave. I have a few officers outside who will detain you. I suggest everyone stay in this room."

Alex rushed over to where Sean stood.

"I'm sorry, but I'm not going to do that when everyone in this room except for you knows that Gordon did this. He's the one who is schizophrenic!"

"Alex!" Sheila called out in surprise.

Sean shook his head and smiled at me.

"You, Alex, will be last," he said and walked towards the study behind Mrs. MacCurdy.

April leaned over and whispered for me to follow her. I stood a little too quickly and felt myself unsteady on my feet. I could feel a small knot forming at the back of my head and it hurt to the touch. I rubbed at my scalp as I left the room with April. As I closed the door, I could hear Alex's protestations and I ignored them. I was actually more worried about losing track of April into Dreamville than my family's concerns.

We walked over to the wide staircase that split into the two wings of the house and sat on the lower step. I took April's hand in mine and kissed it as I stared into her eyes.

"So, Gordon, how do we make all this stop? What is happening to us?"

I shook my head.

"One thing I am sure of now is that I'm not ill. Let me tell you something that I've never told anyone. When the doctors told my parents their diagnosis, they based it on the fact that I told them that I was 25, not 15, and that I was dreaming. What I did not tell them was that I was engaged to a dark haired American woman whose name was April."

April inhaled sharply, but continued to listen.

"When we moved to the states, everything eased up. The hallucinations stopped. I was happy. What no one knew was that I knew you were the woman I loved even when I first met you. You looked exactly like the woman I thought I was engaged to, but I thought your name was Pamela at first. When I heard your brother call you April that summer by the pool, I almost fainted. I think I almost lived at your house that summer, always hoping that you'd notice me."

April sighed and buried her face in her hands, then shook her head as if to shake off the knowledge of what I had just told her.

"I'm sorry, April. Too much?"

She smiled wryly and tilted her head to face me.

"I remember. One of my own trips to Dreamville

involved that summer, except I woke up and I was 32, in a hospital, wearing a pink bikini that I had owned the summer we graduated."

"Yes!" I exclaimed. "I remember. I thought I was hallucinating. I was 25. How could I be 32? How could *we* be 32? I thought it was all my illness. How did you explain it to yourself?"

"I didn't. It seemed as if I was bouncing around in time and space and then I woke up one morning in your bed, engaged to you and you had just told me about your illness. That's why I called it Dreamville, because I thought I had just been dreaming."

"I still don't understand what's going on, Gordon. What's happening to us? I sometimes think I'm ill. Actually, I thought I was always ill and not you. And then suddenly, I forgot my own trips to Dreamville. It was as if my memory had been wiped clean. Until just now, when we were in New York making love and all the memories of Dreamville came flooding back."

"And I knew you knew, too. That was when I found myself back here at Burnock, in the hall with you on the floor."

I looked toward the door and saw the carpet that was

still pushed askew on the floor. Someone had removed the padding. Someone had intended me or someone else to fall there. Maybe someone intent on someone such as Mrs. MacCurdy falling, who might know something she didn't realize she knew. She was always the one who answered the door.

"You know, April, I don't think that fall was meant for me. Who always answers the door? The family never does."

"Mrs. MacCurdy," she said and shivered slightly.

I put my arm around her and pulled her closer to me.

"I'm sure that pad was there last night when you returned because I ran to the door and the rug was steady then."

"It had to have been removed after everyone had gone to bed. No one was here this morning except for myself and Tamara," she said pondering how it might have been removed.

"And the staff."

We sat in silence for a few minutes, mulling over everything that we had just discussed.

"Gordon, there's one problem, well, actually two – Will and Charlotte. Who are they? I've never seen Will and I only saw Charlotte in Dreamville when she introduced herself to me as your fiancée."

I rubbed my temples and thought of Will and Charlotte.

"God, April I have no idea. And you didn't see her in the study. When you were picking up the glass, your hand passed right through her. And Will was in the corner laughing. I was convinced then that I was insane."

"When did I first see them? I saw Will when I was young, but Charlotte, hmm, not till I moved to London, when you went to university. I truly thought she was real. And April, it was awful. I ended up hospitalized. I thought I had lost you forever. I thought she was real and had walked out. I believed I was insane and I fell apart."

"When did you last see them?"

I answered without hesitation. "Today. The New York visit. When I looked down the street, they were at the corner watching the building. Then I looked back at you and saw in your eyes that you had remembered. I decided then to try to break the cycle. In the past version, I had taken you to my apartment. You had looked at me as a stranger then."

"But when I saw that you knew, I took you upstairs.

No matter what age we thought we were, we were as we are now in reality. I wanted to make love to you and break the curse of Dreamville for both of us."

"Have you seen them since?" she asked.

"No, but that's not unusual. I've gone weeks without seeing them and then I've spent entire days jumping back and forth."

"Gordon, could we have broken the cycle? Could we be safe now? Could we have a life, a real life?" she asked quietly.

Before I could answer, I heard loud voices coming from the parlor and grabbed April's hand as we rushed back into the room. What we found there left both of us stunned.

CHAPTER TWENTY-TWO

Alex was standing over the new maid, waving a fireplace poker over her as she cowered in the fireside chair.

"Alex, are you insane?" I yelled.

The sound of my voice seemed to break the trance that was holding everyone else in place and they moved at once to restrain him. At the same time, Sean came running from the study. He grabbed the poker from Alex and placed it back in its stand.

"What the bloody hell do you think you're doing?"

The color had drained from Alex's face and he looked around the room as if he had no idea how he had come to be where he was. It was then that I saw Will step from behind him laughing and heard a gasp from April next to me.

Will was across the room in a second and standing before both of us.

"So now she remembers everything? Too bad for her. I had so wanted to have a go at her. Maybe I still can. Through you. You know, don't you? When things finally end for her?"

April moved behind me and refused to look at Will.

Suddenly Sheila was next to April and leading her to the sofa next to Andrew, the whole time looking at Will.

"Oh ho, someone else sees me," Will said. "Goody-goody. Someone new to the party!" And then he vanished.

Across the room, Sean was trying to sort out the altercation between Alex and the girl as Alex stuttered that he had no idea what Sean was talking about. I realized that no one in the room but April, Sheila, and myself had seen Will. As the others continued to loudly argue over the events, they did not notice as I pulled both Sheila and April into the hall.

"Sheila, did you, well, what did you see?"

April stood back a bit, looking all around the hall as if Will was about to appear again.

Sheila was about to reply when the three of us found ourselves in the study, the day I thought I had pushed Charlotte through the window.

She blinked and looked as if she were about to faint. She had never experienced Dreamville and I'm sure she was wondering if madness were a family trait at that time.

"What . . . where? This is impossible. We were in the great hall and now we're back in the study. How did we get here? And who was that man?" she stammered.

I led her to an armchair and helped her to sit. Her entire body was shaking from the shock of the sudden transposition to Dreamville. April poured her a glass of Scotch and she swallowed its contents in one drink.

"I don't know what to tell you. This has been happening to April and myself for a while, though she had never seen Will before, either. Somehow it's as if time shifts and we end up in the same places, reliving the same events. April calls it Dreamville."

I looked around the room and then back to Sheila.

"It appears that we're back to the day when I thought I had hallucinated pushing Charlotte through the window. We're lucky. It could have been seven years in the future or worse, a decade ago, although none of it is very much fun"

I took the Scotch and poured myself a glass.

"Oh my god, are we mad?" Sheila asked.

I shook my head.

"I have allowed people to make me think I was for over a decade, but it wasn't until April remembered her own travels, that she was traveling with me that I realized I was quite sane."

"I have no idea why you've been pulled into this. Until now, it was just us."

"Well, I want to go back. I don't like this. You're frightening me, Gordon . . ." she paused and then issued a small scream, pointing where Charlotte still lay.

"Who is that? My god, is she dead?"

April knelt beside Sheila and looked in the direction she was pointing.

"You can see someone there?"

"Of course, she looks dead. Red dress. Blonde. Blood everywhere."

Sheila looked up at me.

"Is that, is that Charlotte?"

I nodded and April walked over to the window. She still could not see Charlotte lying with the jagged glass in her throat, the blood clotting in her blonde hair into dark maroon streaks.

"Here? Is this where she is?" April asked. April had no idea that she was literally standing in the center of Charlotte's broken body.

I pulled her away from the window and told her it was.

"Why can you two see her and I can't . . . He's back," she said pointing to where Will had sat laughing the first time this had occurred.

Sheila turned, saw Will behind her and jumped up to move behind April and me.

"I want to go back. I need Andrew. I need to leave," she said and started toward the door.

I took her wrist and pulled her back.

"If we go through that door, we could be back in the hall or still be reliving the other day, or God forbid, enter some other version of Dreamville. But before we do, I need to caution you not to discuss this with anyone, including Andrew. The last thing you need is for someone to think you're insane as they think I am."

"Well, what the hell am I supposed to do? I want nothing to do with this. If we're not insane, we must . . .

oh my god, is this what you've been going through?"

She looked across the room at Charlotte's prone body, but I could see her thoughts accepting the reality of what was happening. She suddenly clasped my shoulders and looked into my eyes.

"Oh, Gordon, I am so very sorry. I have wronged you so. I believed everyone when they told me you were ill. How could I have been so wrong?"

I hugged her and looked sadly at April over Sheila's shoulder.

"It's alright, Sheila, and it will be alright. These 'visits' don't usually last very long. Maybe we can talk later tonight about this. Heaven knows April and I could use someone else's perspective on this."

"Wait, Gordon," April said. "Sheila, sometimes they do last a long time. At one time I was so confused that I actually believed I was 32 and that being engaged to Gordon at 25 was the 'dream'. And once I spent two months with my family as a teenager. It can be very confusing."

April took my arms and wistfully said, "Gordon centered me. Only once was it really bad."

I was stunned. She had remembered the time after

Christmas when I had hurt her, what I had previously thought was really a dream.

"Stop. Don't. That will never happen. Never."

She pulled away from me and wiped a tear from her cheek and started towards the door.

"Well, if we're revisiting the other day, then when I open this door, Sheila and I should go upstairs with you," she said.

Sheila spoke to us as we started to open the door, "Gordon, April, surely you believe that neither I nor Andrew had anything to do with spying on the two of you. You must know that. Especially now."

April took Sheila's hand and moved forward with her.

"Of course, Sheila. Of course."

When they opened the door, they led us not into the parlor, but back into the great hall. I heard Sheila exhale as she opened the door into the parlor where everyone was exactly as we had left them. Sheila's face was pale as she took her place next to Andrew on the sofa. He did not notice her confusion or her trembling hand until she lifted a glass of Scotch and drank deeply.

"Sheila, dear, it's fine. I think Alex has had far too

much to drink and seems unable to explain why he was ranting at the maid."

She smiled at him and took his hand to stop her own trembling. April sat next to her on the sofa and stared around the room. Now that she had seen and heard Will's comments, I could tell that she was more afraid of him than she had ever been of any of the events that had happened in Dreamville.

And I, remembering his words about how it would end, felt a dread in the depths of my gut, a fear that the same miles would continue to be traveled until that horrible dream was allowed to be played out.

I looked to April and our eyes met. She was my refuge and I hers. I only hoped that I would not be her undoing.

CHAPTER TWENTY-THREE

The afternoon turned into evening before Sean had finished questioning all of us. He was exceedingly thorough, even questioning April and myself separately. When he concluded the interviews he gave one more short speech about no one leaving Burnock and giving the person who placed the devices one last chance before he came back with an arrest warrant.

No one spoke and as I escorted him to the door, the others in the room began to disperse into the rest of the house. Even Sheila and Andrew gathered their luggage and carried it back to their room.

Though Mrs. Gregory had prepared a meal for us, April and I found ourselves alone in the long dining hall. Neither of us spoke. Both of us were lost in thoughts of what had happened. We had been sitting there for almost twenty minutes in silence when Samuel and Tamara entered. Samuel gave us a curt nod, seated his wife away from us and went to prepare plates for the two of them. He was still angry over my accusation and I could hardly blame him. But I still did not know whom to trust. Someone had placed those devices. Someone I had, perhaps, trusted.

It was late in the evening when Sheila finally made her way back downstairs. April and I were in the parlor alone, with April lying her head in my lap, neither of us talking of the unspeakable event of which we were thinking. She sat up beside me when Sheila entered the room and sat in the armchair next to us.

"So, now, tell me everything, even the things you haven't told one another. If I'm involved in this, I need to know the complete truth."

April spoke first. She told Sheila everything that she had told me. I reiterated most of what she told Sheila, except for some of my experiences with Charlotte and Will. I hesitated to discuss the more graphic details of the "relationship" with Charlotte, but I did admit that it had been sexual in nature.

"I'm sorry, April. I was younger and I thought you were out of my life. I was angry most of the time and I thought she was a living, breathing person. I even thought the house in Kensington was hers and not mine."

April could not meet my eyes. She hugged a needlepoint pillow of daffodils in a blue and white vase tight to her chest and seemed to be studying the patterns in the carpet. I was afraid that she was either angry or disappointed with me.

"Truly, April, I would never have done it had I known I would see you again."

She looked up at me, bewilderment in her eyes.

"I'm not upset that you might or might not have had a relationship with another woman. It does bother me that you, and now Sheila, are now seeing this woman and I'm not, but that's not the problem. You know that."

Now Sheila was confused.

"What is the problem, other than we seem to be suffering from folie a deux or folie a trois, if there is such a thing?" Sheila asked.

I moved forward on the sofa and could not look at either woman.

"I think it's "officially" called shared delusional

disorder, but I also do not think that's what this is. I honestly have no idea what this is."

I paused before continuing. This was entering painful and dangerous territory.

"April's referring to a dream or "Dreamville" event where I rape her and then murder her at her family's home. Of course, that's after I've murdered her entire family. Oh, and let's not forget the woman and man with me or the fact that her brother Rick isn't really her brother or that her sister-in-law becomes . . . oh my God, Charlotte! How did I forget that?"

Now Sheila leaned forward and gasped.

"Did you just say you murdered April?"

I nodded and then looked up at April's face. She turned away from me and tears were sliding down her cheeks.

"April, love, please don't be afraid. I'll never hurt you. I will love you forever. Please trust me."

She wiped her cheeks and stared at me for a moment before speaking.

"What if it's not you? What if Will "jumps" into you and does it, then leaves you with the guilt and holding a gun in your hand? I'm not afraid of dying. I'm afraid of what you might do to yourself afterward."

"Gordon, don't you see that it's why I subconsciously tried to keep from going to my parents with you, especially with Rick and Lisa there. The memory from Dreamville or the event was so traumatic that I suppressed everything until the other day."

She shivered and hugged the pillow even more tightly to her chest.

"I was blind to it, even the possibility of it, until I saw Will tonight. Now, I'm terrified. We've had a year together and maybe we can't change this, not like we did the other day."

Sheila moved to the sofa and took April and held her.

"April, there is a change you forgot. Me. I've never been in any of these scenarios until tonight. Maybe if you both stay here and don't go back, maybe it won't happen. Maybe that's how we stop it."

I reached over to April and offered her my hand. She took it tentatively at first and then held it firmly. She looked to both Sheila and me and smiled through her tears.

"That's right. We are three now. They are two. We

can change this, maybe even leave Dreamville behind us forever."

We three were happy for the first time that day. And of course, that's when life changed again as we heard a gunshot echoing though the house.

I ran from the room and up the stairs, followed by April and Sheila. I looked down the hall of the east wing and saw Andrew, Samuel and Tamara coming from their bedrooms.

"What the hell was that?" Samuel asked.

I realized that everyone was accounted for except for Alex. I ran to his room and threw open the door. He was lying in front of the fireplace, a pistol in his right hand, and bloody pulp where his handsome face had once been. Across the room from him, Will stood laughing hysterically. Next to him Charlotte stood smiling and next to her, Alex stood looking down at his dead body in confusion.

Behind me I heard screaming and running, but most clearly above everything else, I heard Sheila's voice.

"Oh my God, there are three of them now."

CHAPTER TWENTY-FOUR

I turned around and pushed April back before she could see clearly into the room. I could not allow her to see this. It would be too much for her.

"April, no, go. Shelia, please take everyone downstairs. Samuel, will you remain here with me until the police arrive?"

April pushed against Sheila, struggling to reach me.

"No, Gordon, what's going on. Sheila, stop it!"

Sheila nodded to Andrew and the two of them took April by her arms and forced her back down the hall to the steps. Tamara looked to me and then to her husband. He nodded at her and she followed the others downstairs.

"Good lord, Gordon, why would he do this?" Samuel asked after they were gone.

Samuel could not see the three standing across the room from me. I continued to stare at them rather than look at my cousin's dead body in front of me.

The Alex whose body was lying in the floor walked over to his former body and found himself amazed at what he was seeing. His lips began to move, but no sound came forth. Will looked to Charlotte and smiled. They moved to Alex and vanished with him in tow, leaving his body behind.

I looked to Samuel to see if he had seen any of what had just occurred, but his eyes were transfixed on Alex's body. I would have thought myself completely insane had the remembrance of Sheila's words not reached me, verifying that she, too, had seen what I had seen.

I put my hand on Samuel's shoulder and turned him away, moving us just a short distance from the door to Alex's bedroom.

"Shouldn't we check and see if he's still alive?" Samuel asked. "He might still be alive. We might be able to help him."

I shook my head. "He's gone, Sam. God help him, but there's nothing to be done."

I sat down in a small hall chair and stared at the high

ceiling. For no real reason that I could verify, I knew that Alex had not killed himself and that Will had somehow "jumped" into him and had done it. As Will had two previous times "jumped" into Alex, I felt strongly that he had done it this time as well, though I had no idea where the gun had come from. We had hunting rifles and some antique guns in the house, but not a shiny new pistol like the one that was in Alex's dead hand.

"Did Alex say anything about having a gun?" I asked Samuel. "Had he mentioned any business problems or that he was having trouble with someone?"

"No, he seemed the same vapid ass that he's always been."

Samuel took a deep breath and glanced back towards the half-open door.

"I shouldn't speak ill of him. He was family. I'm sorry. I find it hard to believe that such a self-absorbed man as Alex would shoot himself."

I nodded in agreement, but said nothing.

It did not take more than fifteen minutes for us to hear the distant sounds of the sirens as they neared Burnock. I was fairly certain Sean would be with them.

The ambulance team came first and only remained in

the room long enough to confirm that Alex was dead. Sean came down the east hall, a grim look on his face. He stopped just long enough to exchange a few words with the medical team and then came to where Samuel and I waited.

"Gordon, for the love of God, what is going on here?"

I shrugged my shoulders and ran my hand through my hair.

"Sean, I truly do not know. I was downstairs with April and Sheila when we heard the gunshot. Everyone else had retired for the evening. I found Alex lying in front of the fireplace . . . I didn't check to see . . . to see if he was alive. Maybe I should have."

Sean turned to Samuel who gave a quick summary of the events and where he was when he heard the shot.

Sean sighed and looked into Alex's bedroom where his body still lay.

"Gordon, we'll be here for a while doing our jobs. Have everyone gather in the front parlor so that the other inspectors can question them. You two should go down there as well."

Samuel and I walked slowly down the hall when Sean

called out to me.

"Gordon, this will go far beyond the borders of the village. You should prepare your family for what's about to happen."

"Even if it's suicide?" Samuel asked.

"Especially. Your family is too well known and Alex was well liked. You should start making the appropriate calls."

I raised my eyebrows at that comment. I found it difficult to believe that Alex was that well liked.

"You've been in America a long time, away from Scotland for a long time. I know the two of you have never gotten along very well, but there were many others who thought of him differently. There was even talk of a political career."

I was astonished. Alex? A politician? With his womanizing and his rudeness, he seemed unlikely for such a career.

"I had no idea. No one in the family, including Alex, ever spoke of such a thing."

Sean shrugged as we began to walk to the staircase.

"What can I say? He had quite a bit of influence in Edinburgh and Glasgow. Certainly enough to position himself in the right place to launch a political career."

"My question to you is this – why would a man such as Alex take his own life, a man who had no reason to die?" Sean continued.

It was my turn to shrug. I felt as if I should look back down the wide hall of the east wing, but I did not. I had the strangest feeling that I would see Will, Charlotte, and Alex standing there.

CHAPTER TWENTY-FIVE

I was beginning to believe that we never truly had control over our own destiny. Just as April, Sheila, and I had thought we had come up with a way to avoid the fate that haunted the dreams of April and myself, it seemed as if fate had intervened to bring things to a point that was increasingly unavoidable.

After the police left, after Alex's body was taken away to be prepared for burial in the family plot, after other family members were contacted and the servants prepared the house for the influx of guests for the funeral, I felt empty, useless and helpless. How could I stop what seemed inevitable?

What I feared the most was the fear that April had voiced before the gunshot had echoed through the house

– that Will would "jump" into me and use my body as he had Alex. Or could Alex now do it? Alex hated me and would have killed April to punish me.

I thought of the words I had uttered in the dream about her body being as beautiful and pure as I had thought. Those words were not mine. Those were the words of someone seeing her for the first time such as Will or Alex using my body to extract their revenge. I grew increasingly solitary and began to shut myself away from everyone until the family had gathered for the funeral.

Sean had been correct in his prediction that the tabloids and news media would launch their own investigations of Alex's suicide. Alex was more popular and influential than I had known and when the media could not find answers, they had made them up. Although Burnock was far from the main road, we stopped venturing outside when Sheila had been deluged with reporters and photographers one afternoon in the garden.

I had called Sean and he had arranged for what security he could spare and I had arranged to hire security personnel from Edinburgh, but while I had hoped to have a small private service, his mother and others insisted that the small family chapel was not enough and that a larger ceremony be planned at the parish church for the Church of Scotland of which our family were members.

My aunts and their husbands, distant cousins, and others all notified me of their intention to be there. My father and mother, however, decided their attendance would make the situation worse. After concluding that I was handling things and still managing to cope with my "schizophrenia", father left me to take care of matters as the head of the family. I had no doubt that he believed a great deal of my responsible attitude was due to the presence of April. If I had told him the truth, I knew that he would come to Burnock immediately thinking I had finally and completely have lost my mind. But I saw no use making the situation worse. Better to let him think my medication and April's presence were enough than tell him that April and Sheila were now "infected" with whatever I had seen.

I also recognized that the rest of the family, including Alex's closer relatives were not pleased with my father's absence and my taking his place as head of the family, but they voiced no remarks in my presence. I was still the heir to Burnock, American education or not.

As the houseguests began to telephone their arrival times, I was trying to juggle where to put everyone. Even Burnock had its limits as to the number of guests it could accommodate. Some of the non-family members would simply have to stay in the village, with neighbors, or make the long drive from and back to Edinburgh.

I was sitting at my desk trying to determine these arrangements when April entered the study. She knocked first, which surprised me. She never knocked. She knew that it was an unnecessary gesture for us. We may not have been legally married, but we were closer than some married couples.

"April, is something wrong? You look pale."

She looked out the window toward the garden and then sat on the edge of the Queen Anne chair next to the desk.

"It's so hard to believe that he's gone. Just a few days ago I was riding across the fields with him. He wasn't really bad, Gordon, not when he was himself."

I nodded my understanding as she looked out to the garden again.

"I don't understand why . . ."

She stopped and turned to me.

"My family is flying in, Gordon. I tried to stop them. I really did, but they wanted to be here for you and for me. I'm so sorry. I really tried to stop them," she said as she bent her head and began to weep.

I made my way around the desk quickly and embraced her. I knew what her fears were and they were no different from mine.

"April, it won't happen here. . ." I began, but before I could continue, she pushed me away.

"How can you know that? We don't even know where we'll be or who we'll be in the next minute, much less control some fate that seems destined to happen? Did Alex stand a chance against it? I almost feel as if we're responsible for his death."

She stood and went to the window again, standing with her arms folded as if she were chilled.

"Can you guarantee that it won't happen? That our lives aren't sealed to some horrible destiny? Every time we try to change it, something worse happens."

I went to her and tried to hold her again, but she shoved me this time and I could see an angry fire in her eyes.

"I can't guarantee anything except this – if something happens, you will know it won't be me. I will do everything I can to protect you. I will fight for you, April. I love you. You must believe I do."

She crumpled into my arms and I held her there for several minutes before she could compose herself enough to speak.

"Don't you see, Gordon? We have no control over our lives. It's as if we predestined to live these same fates over and over again. And I'm so angry. I'm furious. It's not fair. Why can't we be like other people and have a normal life?"

I shook my head and watched the fog falling outside.

"Maybe there is no such thing as 'normal'. Who knows? So much has happened in the last years that I sometimes wonder what is real and what isn't. The only real thing I do know is how I feel about you."

"Look, we'll put your family up here. I'll have to shuffle some others around, but your family will be safe here. You will be safe here. I promise."

She sighed and leaned against my chest. It was the only truly private moment we had in the past few days and for the first time we both felt safe in each others' arms. We had no idea that a photographer hidden in the garden had chosen that moment to take our picture.

The next morning Sheila was waiting for us in the dining hall. No one else had descended for breakfast and the houseguests would not begin arriving until that afternoon. She had a newspaper folded next to her plate.

"Before you eat, you should see this. I found it outside the front doors. Prepare yourselves."

She handed us a London tabloid with a picture of the two of us embracing in the study window. It was a beautiful picture, full of our love and the pathos that only we understood. The title and accompanying story, however, were anything but. The headline screamed "The 'Laird' and His Unfaithful Lover" and the article assailed April's American heritage, called her a gold digger, and a disgrace to a good Scottish family. The tabloid was one of the more vicious London ones and I was shocked by how vindictive the article was towards her. But what was worse was the fact that it intimated that there had been an sexual relationship between Alex and April and that she had been unfaithful to me.

She began to shake as she read the damning lies and

she almost fell into the chair next to Sheila.

"Why? Why?" she looked to us and asked. Her breath became ragged and I saw something happening to her that had happened to me on other occasions. She was having a panic attack.

I had her bend her head and talked her through it, trying to help her control her breathing. Sheila quickly poured a cup of Mrs. Gregory's strong coffee and handed it to me. After a few minutes, she had calmed, but she still held the paper in her shaking hands.

"Oh god, Gordon, it's not true. I never. I would never do this."

"I know, love. I know. But Sean warned me this might happen, though I never thought they'd attack you so unkindly."

Sheila had poured coffee for herself and for me and placed the cups on the table.

"Well, someone in the family or the house or the village took money for that tripe," she said.

I became angry at the thought that someone would hurt April to get to me. And the entire story was stupid. We weren't royal Stewarts. We were Clan Stewart, but we were so distant from any nobility that the entire story was almost a joke. A cruel joke, but one nevertheless. The most that could be said of our line was that we had lived at Burnock for centuries and had been distant relatives of the royal Stewarts who went to France and changed the spelling of their family name.

"My family, Gordon, my family will see this," April said.

I shook my head.

"April, where's that American strength of yours? Who cares what these tabloids say? We know the truth. Your family knows the truth and they know the media doesn't care a whit about whom they hurt."

I softly touched her shaking hand and the comfortable calmness of our touch felt like a current moving between us.

"Drink your coffee and I'll get you some oatmeal. Want some cinnamon and brown sugar with it? With a pat of butter and no cream? Right?" I said as I moved to the sideboard with Mrs. Gregory's warm plates of breakfast foods.

She smiled, wiped the tears away and nodded.

"Well, the worst of the day is hopefully over," Sheila said. "We just have to deal with the deluge of visitors and good lord, Alex's mother and her dramatics."

April, always the empathetic being that she was, started to defend Alex's mother, saying that she could understand if the woman was grief stricken.

Sheila snorted and I quietly coughed to hide a laugh as I prepared oatmeal for the three of us.

"April, Alex's mother is only grief stricken if her picture isn't more prominent than other family members. Don't get me wrong. I'm sure she mourns Alex, but you have to remember that Alex learned his manners from someone. No, she'll be a handful, that's certain," Sheila said.

April lay her hand on the paper and traced the outline of our forms in the photograph. She still was very upset by it.

Without looking up she softly said, "You know for the first time, I almost wish I could visit Dreamville when we were kids and escape from this nightmare."

I almost dropped the china bowl and my own hands began to shake. She wasn't thinking of the nightmares that Dreamville had given us.

Before I could speak, Sheila grabbed the paper and tossed it into the large fireplace next to the table.

"No more of that. No more talk of 'Dreamville'. You have some hard times to get through in the next few days. Better to stay grounded in this reality."

"By the way, has anything happened to either of you since Alex . . . Have you 'travelled'? Have you seen anyone? I haven't," she continued.

"Nor have I," I said as I served them their bowls of oatmeal. "Which has surprised me. Will and Charlotte always seem to gloat over bad times. It's strange."

April didn't respond. She seemed as if she were a thousand miles away.

"April?" I asked.

She paused and watched the fire devouring the tabloid.

"Yes. The bad time."

Sheila grasped her hand.

"For god's sake, why didn't you tell us? Why go through it alone?" she said.

April smiled wryly and looked up to me standing at the sideboard. The sun was higher now and was starting to spread its rays through the room. I didn't know it, but I was enveloped in sunlight as they both stared at me.

"What's wrong? Why are you both staring at me? Are

they here?"

"No, Gordon, it's the sunlight. It's as if you're glowing, almost like an avenging angel," Sheila said. "All you need is a flaming sword."

"Don't change the subject," I said, ignoring their stares. "April, why haven't you told me? How long has it been happening?"

"Since Alex . . . died. I don't know how many times."

I rushed to her and looked closely at her cheek. She had covered the bruises with make-up. How had I missed them? Had I been so engrossed in my own world that I had forgotten her?

Sheila was staring at April's cheek now.

"Is that a bruise? How did that happen? Who hit you?"

I sat back in the chair next to April and rubbed my eyes.

"I did. In Dreamville. I did it."

"And April has it here, in reality? That's impossible! How can she be hurt in a dream and have a wound here? That makes no sense," Sheila said.

April laughed.

"How can I get sunburned there and wake up in

New York in winter wearing a pink bikini I owned years ago? I know it doesn't make sense, but it's the way it happens sometimes. God knows I've tried to understand it. If you can explain it, you're better at knowing about Dreamville than I am."

Sheila was stunned by April's words. She looked to me and I turned away from both of them.

"Guess I don't look so angelic now, do I? Tell her everything, April. Tell her before everyone else comes down," I said and left them sitting there.

I started to go to the study and then changed my mind and opened the front door to walk to the garden. I wandered among the trees and the manicured shrubbery before I finally sat down on a bench outside my study window. The morning was damp and the fog seemed to have no intention of clearing. Another rainy, misty day.

Why hadn't April told me that she was reliving 'the bad time' as she called it, over and over since Alex died? I grew angry. Somehow I felt that Will and Charlotte and perhaps even Alex had something to do with her torture. I wracked my brain trying to think of ways to stop what seemed destined and could think of nothing.

As I sat there, I felt someone looking at me and I

turned to see Charlotte standing in the study at the window. She had that Cheshire cat smile on her face and as I turned away from her I found myself sitting on the settee in the Kensington house.

Damn it to hell, I thought. Not now. I closed my eyes so tightly that I could feel the anger exploding with little bursts of light behind my eyelids.

When I opened my eyes, I was again in the garden, but with an incredible headache. Without looking at the window, I rushed back into the house. I was astonished. What had I done to get back? But I didn't care. Anything to escape Dreamville.

CHAPTER TWENTY-SIX

I had no time to talk with either April or Sheila in private as the family, house guests, and local friends of the family began appearing. Mrs. MacCurdy finally gave up on her other tasks and stationed herself in a chair at the front door.

I saw members of the family and locals I hadn't seen since I was a child. After sympathies were expressed, memories began to be exchanged, words of how we had or had not changed. I was glad to see some of them as I had been happy to see Sean again. Why was it that bad things always brought people back together again?

As I spent the day with them, I began to see my life like one of April's mother's crazy quilts. Time and friends and family overlapping and all tied together by the stitching and embroidery that decorated the chaos and uniting it somehow. Something about that image was about to click into place, when Alex's mother, Rowena, made her appearance with a flourish worthy of Gloria Swanson in *Sunset Boulevard*, waiting for her close-up.

Across the great hall I saw April and Sheila with Sean and exchanged small smiles with them. April had no idea what was about to happen, but Sheila, Sean and I all steeled ourselves for Rowena's drama.

Of course, she allowed other family members to embrace and express their grief for her loss first while she tossed her Burberry at Mrs. MacCurdy without even saying a word to the poor woman who had been on her feet most of the day. I made my way around Rowena and went to Mrs. MacCurdy and took the coat.

"Ignore her rudeness. Why don't you go take a break? You must be exhausted."

"But, Mr. Gordon, it would not be proper for someone not to be here to greet your guests," she said in protest.

For the first time since arriving, I noticed how much she had aged since I had last been at Burnock. I had forgotten that she must be nearing 80 and I felt grossly foolish for having treated her so poorly.

"Mrs. MacCurdy, I don't think anyone here has the good manners that you have. Go rest for a while. And tell Mrs. Gregory to take a break as well. Let the temporary people work for a while."

I saw the fear in her eyes and realized that she was afraid she was about to be replaced and I tried to nullify that thought.

"You and Mrs. Gregory are in charge and should tell them what to do. They'll never understand without the two of you to guide them."

Her face brightened and I was glad to see that it had worked.

"Aye, sir, you're absolutely correct. I'll go to Mrs. Gregory immediately. I'm sure she can direct the cooking. Do nae worry. We'll see it done."

As she moved through the crowd of people, I found myself holding Rowena's coat and it reeked from the thick smell of her perfume and cigarette smoke. I threw it on the chair Mrs. MacCurdy had previously occupied and tried to make my way to April, Sheila and Sean, who were hiding their mouths and trying not to laugh.

Unfortunately, Rowena caught sight of me and began

to wail.

"He would not have been here had it not been for Gordon's condition!"

I froze and not a word was spoken as Rowena made her way to where I stood.

"He only wanted to help you! What did you do that would make him so miserable that he, that he . . ." she cried out and waved her arms around to those in the room as if to witness her words.

I sighed and prepared myself for her performance. I wished at that time that I could be as empathetic as April was, but I could not see how this creature was possibly my father's sister. Before I could say a word, however, she spied April almost hiding behind Sheila and pointed a long red fingernail in April's direction.

"And you! Were you the cause of this, you little American schemer? Were you playing the two boys against one another? Trying to get Burnock for yourself? Using Gordon's illness and playing on my poor Alex's sympathetic nature? Gordon, why is she here?"

Rowena's dramatics had gone too far this time. She was almost screaming her spite in April's face.

I had had enough. I placed myself between her and

April and whispered so softly that no one but she could hear my words.

"Enough, Rowena. The performance is over. Andrew and I are going to help you into the parlor where you will behave or you will be escorted to your room where you will remain until tomorrow. Do I make myself clear?"

I could see the anger glittering in her eyes before she suddenly threw herself in my arms and began to wail again. The perfume rose from her as she clung to me, almost taking my breath away.

"My poor, Alex. I'm so sorry, Gordon, April. I'm overcome. Could someone help me to the parlor?"

I nodded to Andrew and he was on Rowena's other side as we led her into the parlor where she could continue to hold court without too much drama. By the time I had returned to the great hall, April was gone and Sheila was making her way to me.

"Kitchen. Thank God you stopped that. We can only hope that was the worst of it."

I thanked her and pushed my way through the small groups from the hall to the kitchen. I found April sitting at the long farm table with Mrs. Gregory and Mrs.

MacCurdy both feeding her tissues as the temporary staff quickly left the room.

"That woman. It would have been better . . ." Mrs. Gregory stopped herself. "I'm sorry, Mr. Gordon. We'll leave you with your miss. Come, Ellie."

It was one of the few times I had heard anyone use Mrs. MacCurdy's first name and I watch as they rose and went from the kitchen to the dining hall.

After they left, I took a seat next to April. She blew her nose, but continued to cry.

"Don't, love. She isn't worth your tears. We tried to warn you that she was a drama queen."

"But everyone will think Alex's death was my fault!"

"They will not. They are far more familiar with Rowena's dramatics than you think. Besides, I stopped it. There will be no more mention of such things."

She wiped her face with one of the tissues and then blew her nose again, this time loudly, which made me laugh. I hugged her and held her head against my shoulder, kissing the top of it.

"That's better." I held her at arm's length and I could see the make-up which had covered the bruise had disappeared into the mound of tissues in front of her.

I touched her cheek with my thumb and leaned in to kiss it.

"You'll want to go up the back steps do some repairs to your make-up. Or you could tell everyone I beat you."

She almost smiled at that and kissed me.

"Not you. I don't know who, but never, never you. I'll be back down shortly. I suppose I do have to go back in there."

She inhaled sharply. "I'm just so glad my family wasn't here."

I returned to the great hall and went to where Sheila and Andrew were talking with Sean. Sean looked a bit angry and I wasn't quite sure why.

"Gordon, why is April's face bruised?" he said tersely.

Before I could speak, Sheila spoke up.

"I slapped her when we found Alex. She became very upset and I was trying to calm her. Gordon was upstairs with Samuel. He didn't know about it until this morning. I was perhaps too heavy handed, but we were all very distraught."

I started to allow Sheila to continue with her lie, but I stopped her.

"Sheila, stop. Sean, I did it. I was having a nightmare and unfortunately she was lying next to me when I swung my arm."

Well, it was almost true. The bruise had come through from Dreamville, from my hand, even if not from me. I waited for Sean to say something and Sheila's face had flushed as she stepped back to lean against her husband.

"Have you been having, ah, episodes?" Sean asked.

This time I lied completely. This was getting very complicated. April, Sheila and I were going to have to come up with plausible explanations. God forbid that April would suddenly walk into the room in a pink bikini and sunburned.

"No, Sean. Considering everything, I've been okay. You can ask Sheila and Andrew or Samuel and Tamara. Hell, ask April. She'll tell you."

He nodded. "I was just concerned. When Rowena began her theatrics, I noticed April crying and a bruise on her cheekbone. I'm going to check on the gate security. I'll be back a little later."

I thanked him and smiled at Sheila and asked her if she would mind checking on April. I knew I had to remain with the rest of the family and guests, although I wanted to be with April more than anything. Sheila agreed and ascended the staircase to the west wing.

An hour passed before Andrew approached me and asked me if I had seen Sheila or April.

"Sorry, but I can't find either of them. Do you think they're okay? I'm just concerned after Rowena's antics."

A shiver ran down my spine and I rushed up the staircase towards my bedroom. I felt my world cave in as I found them tied together in the corner of the room, Charlotte's room.

I whirled around and saw no one else in the room. Outside I could see the dark streets of Kensington. I rushed across the room to them and was untying them when the door began to open. I feared that Will or Charlotte or even Alex would come into the room, but it was even worse. It was Andrew.

"What the hell?" he said and ran over to help me untie them. I don't think he had yet realized we weren't at Burnock.

"Who did this? Gordon, go call Sean," he said as he helped Sheila to her feet when he suddenly looked out the window and saw the damp pavement of the Kensington street.

"What, where . . ."

By this time I had April on her feet and sitting on the gold brocade chaise longue next to the window.

"Will was waiting here when I opened the door. He twisted my arm just as Sheila entered. He grabbed her and tied us together in the floor. We both tried to fight him, but his strength was unbelievable. No matter how hard we hit him, we couldn't stop him," April said.

"A bit like tying two cats together," a voice said from behind us. We all turned to see Will standing in the corner of the room.

"Who is this?" Andrew asked as his face lost all color.

"Your new friend. Oh don't look so sad. I was just about to get Charlotte and Alex, though he's really not being very cooperative. Now you ruined my fun."

Will moved across the room in what seemed like the blink of an eye, placing himself between Andrew and Sheila and April and myself.

"If you want them out of this, then you have to do it. Otherwise they'll end up like Alex. Open up to me, Gordon. It won't hurt, well, not you at least."

I rushed at him and swung out, but found my fist passing through the air as the room shifted and we found ourselves back at Burnock in my bedroom.

April began to weep behind me and Sheila was crying as well. I couldn't find the words to even address what had just happened.

"Will someone tell me what the bloody hell is going on?" Andrew yelled.

My voice failed me and I sat down on the bed which was where April was now sitting instead of a brocade chaise. Will's words echoed through my brain and I clasped April to me as she cried. I noticed that there were rope burns on her wrists and tuned to Sheila. Her skin was unmarked. Why only April? If they both fought him in Dreamville, why had Sheila emerged unscathed and April marked?

"Sheila, you should probably take Andrew to your bedroom and explain what's been happening. After everyone's retired for the evening, come to the parlor and we'll all talk. I'm truly sorry, Andrew. I know it won't make much sense."

Sheila led Andrew from the room and I turned to April.

"We need to cover these bruises and get back downstairs. Sean is already suspicious. He thinks you and Sheila are protecting me, that I've become violent because I'm ill."

As I spoke she had already gone into the bath and began applying heavy make-up to her wrists and face.

"I need to put on pants and socks to hide the marks on my ankles," she said.

"April, I won't do what he said. I don't care what he says, but I don't think he can, well, do anything, not unless I allow it."

She was silent as she dressed in her adjoining room. I followed her in there and waited for her to respond.

"April, I won't. Will you answer me? Please?"

"Gordon, I can't talk about this now. My family will be arriving soon. I can't . . . just leave it for now."

She left the bedrooms and I sat down on her bed and remembered the depravity of being with Charlotte, the bondage, the pain I had inflicted on her at her request. Was that what they wanted my body to do to April? I'd sooner end my own life than hurt her. A thought hit me at that moment. Did they offer that choice to Alex? Torture April or die? If they had and he had refused, then they had killed him. I felt a pang of sadness for my vain, but brave cousin. If he had died to protect April, he was a better man than I had ever imagined.

I rose from the bed and went to the great hall where people were still mingling. I did not see April, but I did not doubt that she was down there somewhere. After about 30 minutes, Sheila and Andrew appeared, neither of them looking too well. Andrew brushed past me quickly, but Sheila stopped and took my arm and spoke in a whisper.

"Give him time. It was a great shock for him, Gordon. Let him find forgiveness."

"Sheila, for God's sake, what happened? April wouldn't even talk and she's hurt. Rope burns on her wrists and feet."

Sheila would not look at me, but I could see a great sadness in her eyes.

"She needs to tell you, Gordon, but it was very, very bad. And I think she thinks she has to die to free you both from this cycle," she said and left me standing on the staircase.

CHAPTER TWENTY-SEVEN

I finally located April in the parlor sitting far across the room, away from Rowena. No one was speaking to April and she looked small and alone in an overstuffed armchair near the fireplace. It was a strange effect as April was much taller than Rowena, but Rowena's presence overwhelmed the room with her theatrics.

Rowena continued speaking as if those people around her were her subjects gathered to hear her divine words. I tried to remember that Alex might have sacrificed himself for April and forgive her airs, but it was very difficult.

It took a few minutes to reach April with so many people coming and going and offering condolences. Just as I found my way to her chair, she jumped up and pushed past me and through the crowd. I turned as she hugged her parents and brothers in the parlor entrance. Her entire family had come, including her brothers and Lisa. I wondered about the baby, then remembered that it would be seven years before Baby David would arrive, if that part of that version of Dreamville came true. But April's brother David was there, embracing her as he and his family looked around the room in confusion.

I saw that they had not expected so many people or for that matter, Burnock, itself. A few locals began to introduce themselves and I saw Sheila and Samuel making their way to April's side. I did not have to see April's face to know that she was crying as she hugged her brothers.

Across the room, next to the front windows, Andrew stood nursing a drink and glaring at me while Rowena was trying to recapture her audience who had been drawn away by the arrival of the American family. Instead of joining April, I went to Andrew. I knew this might be the only time before later this evening to speak with him.

Before I could speak he thrust a glass of Glenfiddich in my hand as he drained his own glass.

"Madness. Either we're all mad or we're in serious trouble."

"I tried to convince Sheila to leave now, to forget the funeral, to go home to our children in Edinburgh and never come here or see you and your cursed family again."

I said nothing, but waited for him to continue. I could tell he was using the scotch to dampen his fears and to stoke his anger. I could not blame him. I wondered for not the first time if I were a curse to everyone who ever cared about me.

He refilled his glass from one of the glass decanters and held it up to me.

"Well, to surviving this damnable place."

When I bowed my head and failed to return his toast, he drained his glass again and started towards his wife.

"Once more into the breech, dear friend. Coming?" he said as he walked away.

April was introducing my family members to hers as Rick moved over to where I was behind the group.

"Gordon, we're really sorry for your loss," he said and shook my hand. "If there's anything we can do . . ."

I shook my head and smiled slightly.

"No, but thank you for coming for April's sake. She's had quite an ordeal. She had become friends with my cousins and with Alex. They seemed to be, to becoming friends of a sort."

"What do you mean?" he asked.

"No, nothing like that. You know April's dry sense of humor and openness. Alex was somewhat like that."

I saw no reason to sully Alex's memory at this time with conjecture or to tell Rick any of the events of the past week. It was enough that only a few of us knew the truth. I took a deep drink of the scotch and wondered if I did tell Rick the truth if he would kill me to save his sister's life.

"I'd just jump into someone else and enjoy the pleasure of it," I heard Will's voice utter behind me. I refused to turn and face him. From now on I would ignore him and Charlotte and even Alex, god help him, if he showed up with them.

But Andrew, unfortunately, did turn towards me just in time to see Will standing behind me. He started to come to where we were when I'm sure Will vanished. He slowed his pace and on reaching us, offered his hand to Rick, all the while looking behind me in search of Will. His behavior was enough to make Rick turn and look.

"Your sister has been wonderful for Gordon,"

Andrew said and Rick smiled.

"Well, Gordon and his parents have been very good friends and neighbors to us as well. We sort of saw the two of them finding their way together eventually, although she certainly was stubborn when we were in school."

"So, you know each other from school?" Andrew said, gesturing with his once more filled glass. I was beginning to wonder how he was even standing at this point considering how much I had seen him imbibe in just a short time.

"Yeah, Gordon and I used to play basketball while April pretended to ignore us, but she always managed to find her way to the pool."

"I cannot imagine Gordon playing basketball, but I can see that he might have used that to get near the pool," Andrew laughed.

"If you will excuse me," I smiled and walked to April while Andrew and Rick continued to talk as Andrew filled a glass for Rick. I could only hope that Rick could keep Andrew's mind off everything until later.

I finally reached April and placed my hand gently at the small of her back. Her father took my hand and shook it as her mother leaned in to hug me and offer condolences from their family. I closed my eyes and wished this evening would soon be over. I was so tired of hearing the phrase 'offer our condolences' that I wanted to walk out into the back fields and scream as loudly as possible. Of course that would seal my reputation as a madman and the thought of that made me almost want to laugh.

Somehow April sensed the tension that was coursing through my body and she placed her arm around my waist and squeezed. I looked down at her and saw that I had been wrong about her tears. She had refrained from crying and I knew it was to hide the bruise that was beneath the thick make-up. She leaned her head against my shoulder and nodded as her family moved into the parlor and began to intermix with my family and the others in attendance.

"It's going to be okay, Gordon. I believe it. We just need to get through the next few days."

I looked into her beautiful dark eyes and prayed that she was right.

Several hours later as the last of the guests had either left or had retired for the evening, Sean came into the house to let us know that he was leaving and that he would have the security in place tomorrow for the services. Other than Andrew, Sheila, April and myself, no one else remained in the parlor except for Rick and Lisa. After meeting Sean and speaking briefly with him, they, too, left to find their room in the east wing.

The four of us sat soberly, none of us quite knowing what to say, when Sheila finally spoke. "Well, we can only pray that a gunshot doesn't interrupt us this time."

CHAPTER TWENTY-EIGHT

"Have you told him yet?" Sheila asked April.

Sheila and Andrew were each sitting across from April and myself and although Andrew was slouched in the armchair, he had recovered from his bout of scotch rather quickly. He must have noticed my observation and he raised the glass.

"Same glass. Weak tea."

I raised my eyebrows in surprise which seemed to set him off a bit.

"You surely didn't think I would get drunk and risk Sheila's life after what happened? I'm not the fool you think I am, Gordon."

I held my hands up and shook my head.

"No, no, I apologize, though I certainly wouldn't

have blamed you for drinking after everything that happened. But Andrew, I've never thought you were a fool. Never."

"Yes, but never as smart as you either, eh?"

"No, Andrew . . ."

How could I explain that my reserve had been a product of my own insecurities and fears or the fact that I thought I had been schizophrenic for over 10 years? I shook my head again and lowered it. If this were any indication of how the evening was about to progress, it told me that any discussion would be futile.

"Andrew, don't be ridiculous. He never said anything remotely like that. Don't be like Alex was. God knows arguing will get us nowhere," Sheila said.

Andrew pulled away from her and looked both angry and hurt, but Sheila knew her husband well.

"Please, Andrew, we can't do this without you."

He took her hand and grimaced, but let some of the anger dissipate.

"April? Did you tell Gordon?" Sheila continued.

It was April's turn to lean back into her seat and look away. Somehow the bruise on her cheek appeared darker. I wanted to reach over and touch her face, but I could tell that she had withdrawn from us this evening. Other than her arm around my waist when her family had arrived, she had barely touched me and had shied away from my touch. Was she afraid of me? What the bloody hell had happened upstairs?

She sighed and began to talk, her voice barely above a whisper.

"I walked into that dark bedroom and lost my bearings. I had never been in that version of Dreamville before and I was very confused. I felt myself being shoved to the floor on my knees and I heard the sound of a zipper."

"I was terrified that something horrible was about to happen and I tried to crawl away when something, someone jerked me back by my hair. The room was so dark. I couldn't see who had hold of me."

She stopped and then looked to Sheila. She still refused to look at me or at Andrew. I saw that for some unknown reason she felt guilty or ashamed of what had occurred.

"That was when I walked in," Sheila said. She must have seen that April was incapable of continuing to relate what had happened.

"The light from the hall illuminated the shape of Will, with April kneeling before him as if . . . anyway, I swung at him, trying to give April a chance to get away from him, but it was useless. Don't ask me how, but somehow he had both of us in the floor in seconds and it felt as if three men were holding us down rather than just him."

Now Andrew was sitting forward, his attention focused completely on his wife's narration. I knew something bad was coming when I saw him pour real scotch into his glass and take a drink of it. Sheila had obviously told him everything.

"I know I scratched him and I even hit his head with mine hard enough to feel as if I had cracked my skull. At the same time, April was fighting him equally hard, but the weight of him, the weight was just too much."

She took her husband's glass and took a drink of the scotch herself and then wiped her eyes with the back of her hand. I glanced at April but she was absolutely still, unable to look at any of us now.

"I have no idea where the rope came from. It was some sort of red nylon cord. Anyway, he tied us both up, but he didn't seem very interested in me at the time.

Instead, he began to . . . he touched April and then pulled himself out and held himself in front of her."

Sheila drained the glass and Andrew refilled it.

"I'm sorry, April. I would have done anything to have stopped him."

I was beginning to get angry.

"Did he . . . April, did he . . ." I asked

Sheila shook her head and reached out to take my hand.

"No, no. He didn't. But what he did do was ugly enough."

Her entire body shook for a moment and Andrew moved closer to her.

"He began to describe what he was going to do. Graphically. Then he said that if you didn't let him, that he would make everyone pay until he got what he wanted."

I was afraid to ask. I knew what she was going to say, but I had to ask anyway.

"What did he say he wanted?"

"April. He said it wouldn't stop until he had her 'completely'."

I shook my head and stood and began to pace.

"No. Never. He's never getting her. Ever."

I went back to April and took her hands in mine.

"I swear this to you upon my own life. He will never have you."

She looked up in my eyes.

"He said he would have me the way you had Charlotte," she said.

I could feel my face flush.

"How can that be when Charlotte wasn't real? I don't understand."

"He said you had had an affair when you came back. He said he wanted that."

"But I didn't. I'm not saying I'm a saint. I did have sex occasionally, but there was no Charlotte, no one like that.

"Then who, Gordon? There had to be someone," she cried.

I began to pace again and tried to think. There had been the one girl. We had gotten into some kinky things, but . . . the red cord. We had used a red cord at the Kensington place. I tried to stop thinking about it. I couldn't think about it. The girl had wanted bondage. I agreed at first, but I couldn't do it. It did not feel good. It wasn't love and all I could think of was April.

I stopped pacing and stared at her. I knew why he wanted her. He wanted her because I was in love with her.

"You know, this has nothing to do with anything that happened in my past. This has to do with April, with how I feel about her," I said.

"Who or what the hell is this thing?" Andrew asked interrupting my thoughts.

"I don't know. One morning he was just there. That was when the strange things started, the schizophrenia diagnosis, the move to the States, and April. I lived every day just to see her in school."

I sat down on the sofa and took her hand again. She did not withdraw from me and instead clasped my hand between hers.

"You got me through a lot of bad days in my teens, though you probably never knew it. As long I could see you, know you were there, I wasn't so worried about everything else."

"Charlotte, or what I thought was Charlotte appeared shortly after I returned to London and you left to go to Columbia. It was a difficult time. I was so far away from you and I was supposed to be better, but I truthfully didn't think I'd see you again so I did see other women."

"I didn't really do anything wrong or illegal. I didn't hurt anyone and I was never serious about anyone."

"So why does this 'Will' thing keep showing up? What is he? Why does he need you or your body, at least, to hurt April?"

April finally spoke up.

"I think there's more to it than just Will. There's the whole Dreamville thing, the time and place shifts. We're all experiencing them. It can't be all Will controlling that as he's not in every version of Dreamville. I think there's much more going on here than just him."

"I think his sudden and very forceful presence is connected to the one event in Dreamville that only Gordon and I have experienced," she said.

I thought about this for a moment and then thought about Alex.

"That would make some sense if it weren't for Alex's death and the fact that both Sheila and I saw Alex standing next to Charlotte and Will immediately after his death."

"You never told me that," April said. "Why did you keep that from me? Did Alex speak? Did he do anything?"

Sheila shook her head.

"No, he just seemed very confused by everything and I don't think anyone has seen him since then."

"I think Alex was actually trying to protect you," I said.

The three of them stared at me in shock.

"I think Will was trying use Alex's body, to force Alex to do what I would not. And after what you just told me about what happened this evening, I don't think Will can do anything to April unless the person he "jumps" into is me, whatever that means. He might be able to make the person harm himself, but not others."

We all pondered that thought – the thought that Will was helpless in hurting April without my consent when Andrew brought up the obvious.

"He can't kill April, but he can force the rest of us to harm ourselves the way he did Alex? That's even more of a reason to get away from here."

April began to shake her head.

"No, I'd rather let the scenario with Gordon happen

than allow another innocent person to die. I'd take my own life rather than allow that to happen."

We all began to argue with her over her statement. I had never told her that I had contemplated ending my own life rather than allowing harm to come to her. Her statement about ending her own life was just as terrifying to me as anything, including my hurting her.

"Absolutely not. That is not even a consideration. And as you said, there's the whole question of Dreamville. It involves more than just the two of us now. You know, earlier I was thinking of those crazy quilts your mother makes with the elaborate stitching and the overlapping fabrics," I said.

"I know this is going to sound absurd, but what if, scientifically or something, the fabric of one reality has overlapped with other ones and Will and Charlotte have found some way to traverse them? It might explain his talk of "jumping" into people here."

Andrew began to laugh.

"Overlapping realities? Crazy quilts? That theory is *crazy*. I don't know what tricks this Will person is using, but he's doing it here. Another reality? Seriously, Gordon, you aren't Doctor Who, well, unless you have a Tardis hidden somewhere. Do you not see how ridiculous you sound?"

Sheila said nothing and blushed at her husband's comments. She had seen more of Dreamville than Andrew had seen and I think she saw some credence in my theory.

But April, April, for the first time, began to see a possible explanation to what had been happening to us. I could see in her face that she thought it might be true, this idea of overlapping realities.

"Haven't there been some scientific theories about alternate realities? Something to do with quantum physics and how the past, present and future are all tied together, occurring simultaneously? I don't know. I could have it confused."

"Yes," I said. "There's so much we don't know. I think one writer said something to the effect that anything scientifically advanced would appear as magic to a less advanced civilization. Sort of like flying an airplane over the Aztec empire. They would try to find an explanation in religion or superstition. We would probably look to science, though some might still look to superstition, I suppose."

"Clarke," Andrew said, surprising us all. "The writer was Arthur C. Clarke. But that's science fiction and it hardly makes any of your Dreamville theories real. Oh, I know, let's all drive down to Stephen Hawking's and toss this ridiculous theory his way. For god's sake, Gordon, you have to stop this."

I sighed and got up and walked to the front windows of the parlor. Outside the fog had surrounded the grounds of the house and it was as if we were the only people in the world, the four of us in that room.

"Well, I can't explain Dreamville any other way. You don't know, Andrew. You haven't been through the things April and I have been through. If you have a better explanation, please tell us all because I'd sooner not see the one woman I've ever loved in this world die. So please! Explain it to us instead of ridiculing everything we say!"

April rose and joined me at the window and held me close. She laid one hand on my burning cheek and kissed me gently.

"Gordon, let's let it go for the night. Come to bed. Even if tomorrow everything ends, we'll have had one last happy night together."

I heard Sheila crying across the room, but looked down into April's clear, certain eyes. She was right. One more good night. We could face tomorrow then. She took my hand and led me out of the room. I never looked back at Sheila and Andrew, although I could vaguely hear their soft voices arguing intensely.

I couldn't think of them or Will or Dreamville or anything but April at that time. Although the house was full of visitors, it held no one but April for me at that moment. When we reached my room, we were quick to undress one another. I drank in the sight of her like a man thirsting in the desert. I just wanted her wrapped around me and to be in her, loving her, and thinking of nothing else but being with her and no one else.

We lost control in one another that night, our love stronger than it had ever been. Although we both knew that the next day might be the end for us, tonight we would be together and we would make it last as long as we could.

And for the first time in months, we were unafraid of Dreamville or what was or wasn't real.

CHAPTER TWENTY-NINE

Mrs. MacCurdy's knock on our door at seven the next morning surprised neither of us. We were awake and expecting it. She informed us through the door that breakfast would be served at eight and then she moved on to the other rooms to perform the same routine.

April and I had not slept and were still wrapped in one another's arms as the sun lightened the sky outside the bedroom window.

"So, it begins?" April asked.

"I don't know. I don't want to leave this bed. I feel we're both safe here – from Will and Dreamville and the whole damn mess."

April took her hand and drew it along my forehead.

"I can see a line forming there that I love in the older

version of you in Dreamville. Have I told you that I love you there as much as I do here, now?"

I smiled and touched my forehead. She was right. A thin crease was beginning. I kissed her forehead.

"No lines on your face. I'll take them for you."

She had surprised me so much with her strength. She had not shed a tear since we came upstairs. Actually, from the onset of our coming here, she had been stubborn and dauntless and she had held my temper in check on more than one occasion. She had simply loved me and had been willing to take on whatever came our way.

I felt so much more frantic. I had to find a way to protect her. Almost everyone would be leaving after the funeral that afternoon except for her family. We knew Sheila and Andrew and Samuel and Tamara would leave immediately. I doubted that Andrew would even allow discussion of staying and risking Sheila's life and I could not blame him. I would do the same.

Once Rowena's circus had concluded and Alex's service was over, she, too, would disappear. That left only April's family and a few guests from London who would be taking the train south on the following day.

April started to rise from the bed and I pulled her

back to me. I would have her one more time. I rolled her on her back and stared into the depths of her dark brown eyes.

"Forever. Whether legal or not, we are together forever. We belong to no other and no other can ever come between us," I said.

"Forever," she replied and led me into her. We made love slowly, lingering over each second with one another as if it were our last. I smiled at her as I watched her face transform with the joy of our lovemaking. Forever.

We did not make an appearance for breakfast and did not make our way downstairs until almost time to leave for the parish church. A few eyes cast curious glances our way, but most everyone respected our privacy. Even her family said little about our failure to appear for breakfast. I wondered if Mrs. MacCurdy and Mrs. Gregory had covered for us in some way, but I really didn't care. I wanted the damned thing over and everyone gone.

Something told me that only then could April and I face Dreamville and the overlapping realities of our world. Until then, we would be brave and hold fast to one another, presenting a united front for both the family and any others.

I had not worn a suit since we had left New York and I found it strange that both April and I had packed funeral clothes without realizing it. She straightened my blue tie and smoothed the shoulders of my charcoal Savile Row suit before we left to join the others. She wore a black Calvin Klein dress and matching coat. We were not surprised to find them pressed and hanging in my armoire that morning. Mrs. MacCurdy's unobtrusive assistance again.

The service was not short, but probably not as long as Rowena would have wished. She made a very dramatic show of her grief, which I supposed could have been genuine. Had I lost my child I could not predict that I would not be equally broken.

The parish church was too small for the number of people who had come to Alex's service, with many people standing outside the open church doors as the minister concluded the ceremony. Once the public services were over, the family and a few guests returned to the small chapel at Burnock where a brief private service took place and where Alex's coffin was interred in the family plot. Andrew, Samuel, myself and three of Alex's friends served as pallbearers. The last part of the afternoon occurred in almost total silence with the exception of an occasional sob from Rowena.

Afterward, everyone returned to Burnock, where after making small talk for a short time, visitors began to depart for home. As each one left, I felt as if more weight was being removed from my shoulders. I was still unhappy with Rowena's need to make the entire ceremony into something that revolved around her and her alone and not about Alex, but I said nothing. As his mother, grief was her right.

It was only as April and I stood next to the door bidding our guests goodbye that I noticed the settee – the settee from our mutual nightmare. I was so taken aback by it that I almost threw the thing out the door immediately, but I refrained and went in search of Mrs. MacCurdy. I could only imagine April's thoughts on seeing it there.

"The settee in the great hall - where did it come from?" I asked when I found Mrs. MacCurdy in the dining hall, overseeing the temporary service staff.

"It was in one of the downstairs rooms we only use for storage. I had it brought to the great hall in case it was needed. It's been there since yesterday, Mr. Gordon," she replied.

"Yesterday?" I was stunned. I was sure neither April nor I had noticed it. She would have mentioned it to me had she seen it.

"Aye, sir. Yesterday morning I had Ferguson bring it in as well as extra chairs before the guests arrived. Is there a problem? I can have it removed."

I could feel my hand shaking and I shoved it in the pocket of my trousers.

"Please have Ferguson immediately remove it from the house. I would appreciate it, Mrs. MacCurdy. Have him take it to the stable. Have him destroy it. I never want to see it again. Make sure he understands that it is to be destroyed. Burned, if possible."

She stared at me as if I were insane, but nodded and left the room to find Ferguson to remove the damnable thing from the great hall. I closed my eyes and tried to regain my composure before returning to the hall. No one but April knew what that settee represented.

I found April in the parlor, sitting with her family and Sheila and Andrew. I smiled at them and joined them there.

"Gordon, I wish we had more time to visit here," April's mother said. "Perhaps after the wedding we can visit. And your parents will be here then as well."

"Mother, Gordon and I aren't sure where we will be after the wedding. We really haven't discussed any of that," April said.

I noticed that Andrew glanced at his watch and then at Sheila, who seemed to be ignoring him.

"Andrew, I suppose you and Sheila must be wanting to start back to Edinburgh. I'm sure you've missed the children."

"Yes, Gordon, but Sheila insists we stay until tomorrow, though Samuel and Tamara are leaving shortly," he said none too happily.

"I'd rather have the day to drive rather than trying to rush back. I feel it's safer that way," she said, pointedly staring at her husband.

I looked to April who I could tell was not happy with this development. I think she wanted everyone gone as much as I did. If we had to deal with Dreamville or Will tonight, we would be better off without having to worry about anyone else being hurt.

"Sheila, I'm sure it will be quite safe to travel this

afternoon."

She shook her head. She wasn't going to budge on this. Damned Stewart stubbornness, I thought.

April's family hadn't a clue as to what was going on, but politely said nothing. It was only when Ferguson and one of the temporary workers began to carry out the settee did anyone say anything.

"Gordon, that's a lovely settee. Why are those men removing it?" Lisa asked.

April's face froze in disbelief. She had not seen the settee until now, which surprised me. She had been standing next to me when I had first noticed it. She and I both turned to Lisa and realized that something about Lisa was not right. Her face, her smile were strangely twisted. It was then that I saw the tiny outline of Charlotte's Cheshire cat smile. Charlotte had jumped – right into Lisa. Would Alex do the same to Rick? Would Will somehow manage to do it to me?

I could see on April's face that she was seeing the events of Dreamville that would lead to her demise on Lisa's face. She turned to face her brother, Rick, to see if any changes had occurred with him. I could discern none, but that did not mean much.

It was as if we were wandering in the darkness, waiting for someone to turn on a light that would reveal the final horrors of Dreamville. Sheila watched us and could tell that something was not right, but she knew little of Charlotte and Andrew knew almost nothing.

"Gordon, why don't you take April upstairs? She looks very tired from today's events."

"Excellent idea, Sheila. We should all get some rest tonight as tomorrow will be rather hectic."

I took April's hand, bid everyone good evening and led her from the parlor. Just as we were about to go up the staircase, Rick followed us into the hall and placed himself between us and the steps.

"Gordon, they've told me you have to let her go."

Both April and I realized that we were not speaking with her brother, but Alex instead.

"Alex?" she asked quietly. "Where's my brother? Where's Rick?"

Alex shook his head.

"I believe he's still in here. I don't know how they do it, but they can with everyone but the two of you. For some reason, they can't jump into you two as they do others. I think you have to allow them to do it, but the rest of us . . . The one man killed me and made it appear as if I had done it."

"The man is very, very angry. I don't know why. All I can tell you is what he told me to tell you. I'm sorry I couldn't stop him. I did try and I did keep him from using me to hurt you, April."

April moved forward and hugged her brother, knowing that Alex was in there with Rick. I had a sudden thought and I prayed that Rick was not aware of what was happening.

"Alex, tell us what you can. Who are they? Why the time shifts? The jumps? How did you 'jump' into Rick? Help us, please," I said.

Again, Alex shook his head.

"I don't know. I was somewhere else. I can't remember where. And then they pushed me into this person. Rick? Is that his name?"

April and I nodded in unison.

"The time shifts and the place you call Dreamville. I don't understand. It's as if when I'm here, my memory is wiped. All I can tell you is that these two – Will and Charlotte? They want April dead and I can't help. I can feel him coming. Gordon, I'm sorry. Truly. I don't think you can stop him."

"Alex, for god's sake, fight him. Help us."

But as I spoke the words I could see Alex vanish from Rick and see Rick's confusion as to how he had come to be standing next to us. I was at a loss to explain, but April, my love, was unafraid and tried to help her brother. By the time she had aided him and convinced him to rejoin the others in the parlor, I had finally regained my own composure.

When we saw that he had left the great hall, we ran up the staircase to my room. I was half afraid that we would open the bedroom door to the Kensington house, but Dreamville was not awaiting us on the other side of the door, just my room as we had left it that morning.

"I've got to get out of these clothes," April said and went to her adjoining bedroom to change. I decided to change as well and grabbed a pair of jeans and an old rag wool sweater. As I changed, I mused aloud to her as to what Alex had revealed to us through Rick.

"Don't you think that their inability to 'jump' into us has to do with our free will?" I called out to April.

I heard no response from her and heard no movements in her bedroom. I walked through the open room and found her gone. Only her black dress and coat lay on the bed. I could feel panic knotting my gut.

"April, answer me. Where are you? April? April!"

The silence of a vacuum was all I found.

CHAPTER THIRTY

I searched both our rooms but could find no evidence that she was ever there except for the dress and coat. No other clothing. No toiletries. No luggage. Nothing.

I sat on her bed and buried my face in her dress and could smell only the very faint delicacy of Chanel No. 5. I held my breath and I prayed. I looked out the window of her bedroom and saw the heavy frost on the ground and realized that it was early morning rather than early evening.

I tossed the dress aside and ran downstairs to find the house empty. The great hall, the parlor. All guests who had been there earlier were gone. I remembered the staff and went to the back of the house to see if Mrs. MacCurdy or Mrs. Gregory were there.

Instead of them, I found only an older woman I had never seen before at the stove stirring a small pot of oatmeal.

"Sir, I didn't know you were about yet. I'll have your breakfast ready in just a few minutes."

I stared at her, which seemed to unnerve her a bit.

"Is something wrong, sir? Do you need Craig to bring the car around?"

I realized then who she was – the new girl who had just started working at the house in the past few weeks. But now she was much older. Almost 25 years. And who was Craig?

And then it hit me. Dreamville. I had travelled forward, but this time much farther than I ever had in the past. If the girl looked 25 years older, how old was I? I rushed from the kitchen to the parlor where a mirror hung and I stared at my reflection in shock.

My face was lined and my hair, though still full, was turning white. I had to be in my late forties, possibly 50. Instead of touching my own face, I touched the lined visage in the mirror before me. How could this be?

I thought of April's clothing on the bed upstairs and wondered why it was there. If I had travelled to a future

Dreamville, I could think of only one reason why her dress was there and she was not and that reason made me double over in pain.

God, no, I thought. She had to be . . . She couldn't be . . . gone. I was afraid to face what might be a possible future, but I had to know. I slowly walked out the front doors into the cold air and across the lawn to the chapel and the churchyard. The chapel was in horrible shape. In one place the roof sagged and appeared ready to crumble. Glass was missing from some of the windows and a chain was attached to the door with a heavy padlock on it.

I turned back to look at Burnock and round it equally in disrepair. The east wing looked shuttered and the roof of the entire building was also in poor shape. I realized that I was walking through weeds and noticed that the lawn was no longer cared for and that thistle had found purchase in places where a manicured lawn once existed. Where the formal garden had once been was now an overgrown patch with actual brambles and large trees blocking access to it. Only the path to the churchyard seemed to still exist as if someone had made more than a few trips from the house to it.

One step closer and I would be in it. I was so afraid

of what I would find there. I saw Alex's monument, now covered in moss and aged where today it had been shiny and smooth. Next to it I almost wept to find a small tomb which held the remains of my parents. It was newer, but still stained with at least ten years of Scottish weather.

I moved down the path and I knew in my heart what lay beyond it. I fell to my knees before the stone which was almost as old as Alex's monument and reached out my hand to trace the name there. Pamela April Norris Stewart. A cairn stood next to it and a small handful of stones. I placed one of the stones atop the cairn, carefully balancing it. It was the old way, before tombs and more modern monuments. Someone, possibly me, came here and kept her memory fresh by placing the stones upon the cairn.

I saw below her name a faded date that read January 8, 2012 and the words Beloved Wife and below that a single word – Forever.

I almost lie prone on the heavily frosted ground in front of her stone and wept. How had I not stopped it? I looked again at the monument and saw that it read Stewart. It had not happened the night of Alex's funeral.

We had married, though I knew not when. But we had had a short time together. Alex had died in the spring of 2011.

I pulled myself together and touched the top of her monument again as I stood. I looked all around and tried to remember that I was possibly in Dreamville. Maybe Dreamville was giving me a warning, a way to stop the prediction engraved in the stone before me.

I could save her. I would marry her. I would save her.

I ran to the house and I cried out to the heavens, to her.

"April, love, hold on. I'm coming. Hold on."

I would not let her die in any world. Not in Dreamville. Not in our real world.

She would live.

ABOUT THE AUTHOR

Reneé Porter is the author of the series of novels, **The Taliaferro Chronicles**, including *The 13th Victim, Redemption Ridge*, and *An Inquisition of Angels,* as well as the novels *Bell Park* and *Dreamville. Gordon's Dream,* the sequel to *Dreamville* is her sixth novel.